The Diary of Melanie Martin

or

How I Survived Matt the Brat, Michelangelo, and the Leaning Tower of Pizza

BY

CAROL WESTON

A Yearling Book

Published by
Dell Yearling
an imprint of
Random House Children's Books
a division of Random House, Inc.
1540 Broadway
New York, New York 10036

Visit us on the Web! www.randomhouse.com/kids

Educators and librarians, for a variety of teaching tools, visit us at
www.randomhouse.com/teachers

ISBN: 0-440-41667-1

Reprinted by arrangement with Alfred A. Knopf, a division of Random House, Inc.

Printed in the United States of America

June 2001

10 9 8 7 6 5

OPM

To my muses,
Emme, Elizabeth, and Robert Ackerman,

and my extraordinary editor,
Tracy Gates

ITALY

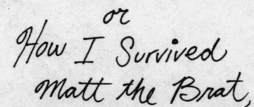

The Diary of Melanie Martin

or

How I Survived Matt the Brat, Michelangelo, and the Leaning Tower of Pizza

home in bed

Dear Diary,

You will never in a million years guess where we're going.

Nope. Guess again.

Never mind, I'll tell you. Italy! We're going to ITALY!

In Europe!! ACROSS THE OCEAN!!

I even have a passport. It's really cool except I'm squinting my eyes in the photo, so I look like a dork.

At least that's what my brother said. I call him Matt the Brat. You would too.

Trust me.

He is so annoying it's not even funny. He copies me, hides my hairbrush, brags that he has no homework, and spies on me when I have friends over. When he's extra annoying, I'll hit him lightly, he'll cry, and then *I'll* get in trouble.

Or take tonight. We went out for Chinese food, and I ordered beef and broccoli. Sometimes I use chopsticks, sometimes I use a fork, but I always eat all the meat and only one broccoli—two if Mom is watching. Anyway, after I drank up all my Sprite, Matt took his straw and started blowing bubbles into his. Really loudly. I said, "You are so disgusting!" He smiled and said, "I know." And Mom beamed at him like he's so adorable.

He *used* to be adorable. Back when he was a newborn, six years ago. I guess he must still be kind of cute because everyone always makes a fuss over his blue eyes and long lashes and dinky freckles.

People used to call me cute too, but they don't anymore. No one notices me much.

I don't mind. Who wants to be called cute when you're already ten?

Okay, maybe I mind a little. I miss when people called me cute and I didn't have homework and no one expected me to set the table or put away dishes or make my bed or act my age.

Mom reminds me that now that I'm older, I get an allowance. Four dollars because I'm in fourth grade. Sounds good, right?

Well, half the time she forgets to give it to me and I forget to remind her. Then when I do say, "Mom, you must owe me twenty dollars by now," she'll hand me just four and tell me she's always buying me stuff.

Like this new diary, for instance.

Anyhow, Dad got a bunch of frequent-flier miles because he frequently flies for his job. He said we could all fly somewhere for free, and he let Mom pick where. She picked Italy because it's full of art and she loves art.

She even loves teaching it. She teaches in the middle school on Monday, Tuesday, and Wednesday. It can be embarrassing having Mom in the same building as me. Like when she waves or wears something weird or talks to my teachers or puts her arm around me in the hall.

But I like knowing she's close by.

Right now we're both counting the days until spring break.

Uh-oh, it's already ten—like me! I better turn out the light.

Yours truly,

Melanie

Dear Diary,

BAD NEWS. I told Miss Sands that my family was going to Italy for ten days and that since the planes were full on the weekend, we'd be leaving next Thursday afternoon, so I'd miss one and a half days of school. Big deal, right? One and a half puny days. I expected Miss Sands to say, "Italy! Lucky you!" or something.

But she didn't. She said that in Social Studies the class will be doing a chapter called "The Family," so while we're away, she wants me to think about my "place in the family." She also said I'll have to write a poem and bring in postcards to share with my classmates.

Miss Sands can be so strict. Family? Who does she think I'm taking the trip with? Friends? Strangers? It would be impossible *not* to think about my family! And postcards sound okay—but a poem? How will I know what to write?

I asked her if it could be short, and she said to make it at least thirty lines.

Thirty lines!

I wouldn't mind writing a haiku or a limerick—but thirty lines!

Miss Sands has been teaching us poems by Edna St. Vincent Millay and Langston Hughes and Shel Silverstein. Sometimes she makes us memorize poems. The one I memorized was by Robert Louis Stevenson. It has two lines:

> *The world is so full of a number of things,*
> *I'm sure we should all be as happy as kings.*

I *was* as happy as a king (or queen), except now I'm starting to worry about writing that stupid poem.

Mom says I worry too much.

I'm even a little worried about going away.

I mean, I've never flown over the ocean. And I've never spent ten days nonstop with just my family and nobody else. And I've never been to a faraway place where the food is different and the language is different and everything is different. And who am I supposed to play with for all that time? Matt? Usually I spend half my vacation in my jammies hanging around the apartment *avoiding* Matt. The other half I spend at Cecily's.

Cecily is my best friend. She and I have been friends since kindergarten. She lives with her mom about ten blocks away. She has a bunny who bites and a cat who purrs. Cecily and I have the exact exact exact same taste in boys. Right now we both like a boy named Christopher.

It can be bad when two friends like the same boy. In our case it's not, though, because Christopher never says hi to either one of us.

Not only do we like the same boy (Christopher), but we hate the same boy (Norbert).

Norbert's new, and nobody really likes him. He just moved to New York over Christmas. (I forget where he's from. Cecily says Mars.) Even his name is weird. Norbert. He never talks much, and he has a little bit of an accent. One time he was talking about a magazine subscription and said, "Ten issues for fifteen dollars," and everyone thought he said, "Tennis shoes for fifteen dollars." We all laughed, but later when I told Mom about it, she defended him saying that "ten issues" and "tennis shoes" do sound a lot alike. (Sometimes Mom just doesn't get it.)

Cecily calls him Nerdy Norbert. She said he once picked his nose in the library—and ate it—but I really don't know if that's true. Norbert is tall with brown eyes, and his hair always sticks up in the back. That *is* true. He has a bad hair day every day. Plus his shirts are purple and orange and green, which is too rainbow bright. And his backpack has a pair of fuzzy dice dangling from it. How out is that?

Anyway, I'm going to miss Cecily when we're in Italy. Ten days with nobody to hang out with except Matt the Brat! What if I die of utter boredom? What if Matt annoys me to death?

Worrying,

Melanie

in the kitchen

Dear Diary,

School was so so so embarrassing today! At lunch there was a potato bar so I asked for a baked potato with bacon bits, and I also got peach slices and milk. But somehow I tripped and fell and dropped my tray, and my potato rolled off and the milk splattered, and as if all that wasn't bad enough, it was Norbert who came running over to ask if I was okay and to help me pick up my potato and everything. I wish I could have flown away to Italy that very second.

Mortified,

Mel

March 18

bedtime

Dear Diary,

Tonight Dad and I couldn't find Matt anywhere. Mom was at a meeting, and Dad and I were calling "Matt! Matt! Matt!" at the top of our lungs.

When Matt finally walked in, Dad yelled at him (hee hee). Matt had gone up in the elevator of our apartment building by himself *without asking permission*. He said he wanted to say good-bye to Lily. Lily is in first grade with him and she and Matt are madly in love.

At bedtime Dad tucked me in but left the light on so I could write. I kind of like it better when Mom tucks me in, even though she can be too mushy and says stuff like "Sleep tight, Precious" and "Sweet dreams, Sweet Pea."

Lately she's been teaching me Italian words. Some words are easy. Like spaghetti is *spaghetti* (Spa Get Tee). Impossible is *impossibile* (Im Po See Bee Lay). But most words are hard. To say good morning, you have to say *buon giorno* (Bwone Jor No). Good night is *buona notte* (Bwo Na Note Tay).

The reason why Dad tucks me in faster than Mom is because he usually has work to do or a book to read or a game to watch. Tonight, though, he sat on my bed and started talking. He said he is counting on me to be well behaved in Italy. He said he expects me to help take care of Matt because it's a big deal that we're going

9

overseas and most parents in their right minds would not take kids with them on such an adult trip. He said that since Matt is always wandering off, he wants me to help keep an eye on him.

I'm excited about going on a grown-up trip and everything, but I *am* still a kid. If Mom and Dad can hardly keep track of Matt, what makes them think I can? Sometimes I can't even keep track of my glasses or homework or stuffed animals.

I hope I'll be able to fall asleep.

Here's a poem I wrote:

One more day till
We're on our way—
Doesn't that seem
Im Po See Bee Lay?

Yours,

M. M.

on board!!!

Dear Diary,

We're on the plane, and we're about to take off, and I have to go to the bathroom really really really badly, but the Fasten Your Seat Belts light is still on.

I told Mom, and she said I should have gone at the airport when everyone else did.

Thanks a lot, Mom.

I can't believe I'm stuck sitting next to Matt for eight whole hours. At least I got the window seat. Matt has the airplane headphones on. He wants to play Go Fish, but we have to keep our tray tables in the upright and locked position. I'm a little old for Go Fish anyway.

Plus I'm about to pee in my pants.

I wish we would take off already.

We're up in the air. Outside I saw the tops of sky-scrapers, and now I can see a whole blanket of clouds. It looks like snow out there. It looks like you could put on boots and go tromping around. I showed Matt, but it worries him to be up so high—he keeps asking me to pull down the window shade.

He also keeps asking me to play Twenty Questions. I'd be happy to play Twenty Questions with a normal person, but Matt always picks Snoopy or Bamm-Bamm or Tony the Tiger, and then he can't even answer the most basic question, like "Dead or alive?" or "Man or woman?" Talk about pathetic.

Dad came over and showed us a map in the airline magazine. Right now we are flying over the Atlantic Ocean. Next stop: Italy!

But first there's going to be a movie.

I finally went to the bathroom. When I got to the back of the plane, one door said Vacant and one said Occupied, and for a second I wasn't sure which meant what, but I figured it out and went in the vacant one.

Good thing there was a vacant one.

It was a close call.

It was also a tiny little bathroom, and when I flushed, the noise was so loud, I almost freaked out.

Matt and I have already played War and Crazy Eights, and now he's coloring and making puppets out of barf bags. I used to like to do that. Now I'd rather play Hangman with Mom, but she's sitting with Dad. He's organizing his new travel wallet.

The flight attendants gave us little bags of pretzels, and Matt tried to make his bag last longer than mine, but I hid my last pretzel, so I won. We are about to have dinner. I hope it's Chinese food.

It wasn't. It was salmon or chicken, so I ordered chicken, but it was rubbery white chicken (I like dark meat) with disgusting mushroom gravy. Also, the fork and knife were freezing cold. Also, the plane started bumping up and down, and that made Matt spill some of his peas, and a few landed on me.

The pilot said the bumps were because of air pockets. Pants pockets, I understand. But air pockets? Matt gripped my arm so hard, he left fingernail marks. I was tempted to yell at him, but I didn't since he was scared. Dad said we probably just bumped into a cloud. Then he told me to pass my chicken if I wasn't going to eat it. (Sometimes Dad can be a Big Pig.)

I hope we don't run out of gas up here.

Mom told me not to worry. She also made us ask for milk, which I didn't think was fair considering there was Sprite and Mom and Dad asked for champagne. The champagne was free because we're on an international flight.

I hope Mom and Dad are not drunk. They're all smiley and stuff. They keep saying this trip is like a honeymoon—only with kids. Their anniversary is next week. They have been married thirteen years.

Uh-oh. Thirteen is an unlucky number!

Mom and Dad are now asleep.

Matt is too. He looks goofy because his mouth is wide open.

I'm too excited to sleep. Mom told me to try to sleep so I don't get jet-lagged.

You see, when we left New York, people in Italy were *already* asleep. And when we arrive, even though to us it will feel like the middle of the night, in Italy it will be the morning of a new day. Why? Because the sun rises in the east, and we're flying east.

Maybe I will try to sleep after all. I hope I don't miss the movie.

Buona Notte!
Mel

March 20
in a car
morning, but it feels like night

Dear Diary,

I missed the movie. I woke up right when we landed, and my ears were plugged and I could barely hear, but they finally popped while we were standing around waiting for our luggage.

Right before they popped, I could hear gurgling noises inside my head. I could also hear Matt asking, "Why is it taking so long to clean our baggage?"

Get it? Baggage *claim*? Baggage *clean*? What a dumdum. Like people were really back there scrub-a-dub-dubbing our luggage for us.

When we got our baggage in Rome—excuse me, *Roma* (Ro Ma)—I dug out Hedgehog, and Matt dug out Dog-

Dog. I love Hedgehog so much. She is the fluffiest, softest, cutest stuffed animal ever. Matt loves DogDog too. DogDog is tan with big floppy ears. Matt thinks DogDog sleeps all day and guards him all night.

I must admit that our trip got off to a pretty bad start.

After claiming our baggage, we had to go through customs and show our passports.

Mom said, "Don't you have them, honey?"

Dad said, "No, sweetheart, you have them."

Mom said, "I don't think so, hon."

Dad said, "Sweetheart, I'm sure."

Whenever Mom and Dad call each other "honey" and "sweetheart," you can tell they're annoyed.

Well, Mom started looking in her purse, and Dad started looking in his travel wallet, and they both started looking in their pockets, and Matt started looking like he was going to burst into tears.

And then he did.

It didn't help that to all of us it felt like the middle of the night.

To distract Matt, I said, "Did you know that I have a magic tongue?"

Matt said, "Do not."

I said, "Watch this."

I pressed my nose, and out popped my tongue. I pulled my right earlobe, and my tongue pointed right. I pulled my left earlobe, and my tongue pointed left. I pressed my nose again and made my tongue disappear.

"See?" I said.

Matt smiled, and I felt like a good big sister, except then I noticed these two girls who looked like fifth graders staring at me as though I were an alien. I was completely embarrassed.

Just then Mom found the passports, dorky photos and all.

Matt and I said, "Hurray!" but Dad just said, "I knew you had them." He was being a grump, and I didn't know whether to try to cheer him up or keep my distance.

We got back on line, and the customs people stamped our passports, checked our luggage, and let us in.

To Italy!

The first thing Mom and Dad did was go to an airport coffee shop. Mom ordered *due cappuccini* (Doo Ay Ca Poo Chee Nee), which means two cappuccinos. Then Mom told the waiter it was *delizioso* (Day Leet See Oh Zo), which means delicious. She said it over and over. You'd think it was Gummi Bears or M&M's the way she was acting.

I think Mom just likes to practice her Italian. Almost everyone here speaks Italian—even kids. Except the tourists. They speak English and Japanese and German and French and other languages too.

People seem nice, but I don't know what anyone is saying, so I can't eavesdrop, which stinks because I like to eavesdrop.

Mom and Dad ordered us apple pastries, and I wolfed mine down. Matt was too sleepy to eat his.

Mom said, "Matt, you didn't touch your pastry." So Matt touched it by poking it with his finger.

Matt can be pretty cute sometimes. Or dumb. It depends on my mood. Last year at a Japanese restaurant, the waiter gave us hot washcloths for our hands, and Matt took off his sandals and started using his washcloth to clean his feet! Mom and Dad yelled at him, but I thought it was kind of cute and kind of dumb.

Mostly, though, I think Cecily lucked out since she's an only child.

Anyway, we rented a car, and it cost one million *lire* (Lee Ray)! One million *lire*! Think of all the M&M's you could buy with that much money!

I was worried we were going to run out of money before we even started our family honeymoon, but Mom said things are not as expensive as they sound and we brought enough.

I hope so. I didn't bring any. Mine is scrunched up in my kitty bank in New York.

Well, we are now in the car driving north to Tuscany for four hours. We'll spend four nights at a hotel and take little day trips.

Mom is looking out the window. She is saying things like, "Do you see those cypress trees?" "Isn't that a pretty vineyard?" "Look at those magnificent old olive trees!"

I'm *trying* to look.

Matt's just sleeping with his mouth hanging open. I hereby nominate him for Dork of the Year award.

Dad says he can't concentrate on the countryside because Italians drive really really really fast. Like a hundred miles an hour. Except they use kilometers, not miles. So far, Dad has cursed three times (the H curse once and the

D curse twice). The first two times, Mom frowned and said, "Honey!" The third time, she didn't say anything.

Personally, I can't believe I'm spending eight hours in a plane and four hours in a car today. That's twelve hours—and a day has only twenty-four.

If I were Sabrina the Teenage Witch, I could have gotten here by magic. If I were Judy Jetson, I could have gotten here in minutes. But I'm just plain Melanie Martin, and it took forever to get from home to Rome.

Hey, that's another poem! I'll call it "Romeward Bound" (like "Homeward Bound").

My family went
from home
to Rome.

With Love from ITALY,

MELANIE

in a pensione near Pisa

Dear Diary,

I showed Matt my poem.

He said it was stupid.

I say he's stupid.

We're at our hotel, but it's not really a hotel. It's more like a B&B, or Bed and Breakfast, only here it's called a *pensione* (Pen See Own Ay). You see, there's this nice lady, Paola (Pow La), who lives in a giant house, but her kids are all grown up, so now she makes money by renting out rooms. Our room is big and has two beds, one for Mom and Dad and one for Matt and me. It also has a desk and a chair and a radiator and lacy white curtains. Outside, you can see lines of cypress trees. They are tall and skinny and shaped like candle flames. You can also see pear trees with white blossoms. And a vineyard, even though the vines have no grapes yet.

My only complaint is that I wish our room had one of those little hotel refrigerators in it.

I am so sleepy, but Mom and Dad say we have to

push ourselves to get on Italian time. They say we're not allowed to go to bed, because here it's only four in the afternoon.

Can you believe I have been begging to go to bed?

Dad said we should go see the Leaning Tower of Pisa (Pee Za).

Matt said, "The Leaning Tower of Pizza?!"

I said, "*Pisa*, you moron. But I don't want to go. I'm too tired."

Mom said, "You have to, because we can't leave you alone."

I said, "I don't have to do anything I don't want to do."

Dad said, "You most certainly do, because this is a family trip. Don't you remember our little talk?"

I said, "Well, I'm staying in the car, because I'm pooped."

Dad said, "Suit yourself."

Can you believe we are going to get back in our car?

Mom said, "You'll get your second wind."

Dad said, "It's okay with me if she wants to miss one of the most famous buildings in the world."

Matt said, "I'm not one bit tired."

Well, of course Matt isn't! He's been napping like a newborn!

Tired as h—ll,

Mel

same day
in the car again

Dear Diary,

Dad parked the car very near the Leaning Tower, but I'm still not getting out.

I'm just going to sit here all alone.

I'm just going to wait in this new-smelling car with the doors locked until they come back.

I sneaked a peek at the Leaning Tower of Pisa.

It's big and lopsided and all tilted over. It looks fake. Disneylandy.

People aren't allowed to climb up it anymore, but I wouldn't mind going a little closer.

What should I do?

If I stay in the car, I'll miss everything.

If I hop out and say, "I got my second wind!" I'll be embarrassed.

DAZed and confused,
Melanie

same day

in the *pensione* again

Dear Diary,

Matt came and got me! He was all out of breath and said, "You gotta see this!" I grumbled and sighed and made a big production out of getting out of the car and said, "Oh, fine," as though I were doing him a big favor (hee hee).

The Leaning Tower of Pisa is soooo cooool. It is in the *Campo dei Miracoli* (Cam Po Day Ee Me Ra Co Lee), which means Field of Miracles. It *is* kind of a miracle that it hasn't keeled over and crashed once and for all—*kaboom!*—like the skyscrapers Matt makes out of blocks.

What happened was that hundreds of years ago,

some builders made a terrible mistake and built a tower on sandy clay instead of solid ground. It didn't start leaning until they were working on the third story, and by then they didn't want to stop.

Dad read that in his guidebook. He's always reading. Even at home he likes reading big fat books in his big soft chair.

Well, guess what? The mistake turned out great because people like leaning towers even more than straight ones.

Mom gave me a thousand *lire* so I could buy a postcard for school. Hurray! My first postcard! (A thousand *lire* sounds like a lot, but it's less than a dollar.)

Mom and Dad also gave Matt and me each a disposable camera, and Matt has already used up almost all his film. He took some funny pictures of my feet and his feet. And my nostrils and his sunglasses. And my elbows and his knees. And lots of birds—mostly pigeons. I was in the middle of posing as a human bridge, but then I saw an Italian boy who looked a little bit like Christopher, and he smiled at me, and I could feel my cheeks get all red.

Dad started lecturing Matt about saving film for the rest of the trip. But Mom must have thought Matt was being *artistico* (Are Tees Teek Oh), because she defended him and said, "It's his camera, Marc."

Dad's name is Marc. Mom's is Miranda. All our names start with M: Marc, Miranda, Melanie, Matt.

Don't ask me why.

I took only three pictures. In one, I made Matt lean the same way as the tower. In the other, I made him lift his arms so it would look as though he were holding up the tower. In the third, I took a picture of Mom and Dad—but Dad put one hand behind Mom's head and made rabbit ears.

I Love Being a Tourist!

Your friend,
Melanie

first day of spring

driving to FLORENCE

Dear Diary,

I HATE BEING A TOURIST!

Why did I think that going to Italy would be fun? All I wanted this morning was to be left alone so I could sleep sleep sleep, but Dad said we had to get up to go "exploring."

Dad was halfway dressed. He was wearing striped boxer shorts and black kneesocks. He looked funny. I was going to make a joke, but I thought he might get mad. He gets mad too much, but Mom defends him and says it's because he works so hard. He's a lawyer, which means he argues for a living. Mom works hard too, but she doesn't get mad as much.

Anyway, Mom made me take a quick shower when she knows I like baths better—especially now that I never have to take them with Matt anymore. (I used to worry he would tinkle in the tub.)

Well, I took my shower, but at first I couldn't figure out the hot and cold knobs because they don't say H and C, they say F and C, and the C isn't for cold, it's for *caldo* (Cal Doe), which means hot. I practically burned myself to death before I got it straight.

As I was drying off, I noticed Mom's makeup bag just sitting there. I wiped the steam off the mirror and put on lipstick and eye shadow and blush.

I wonder if Christopher would notice me if I wore lipstick.

I wonder if he's noticing Cecily while I'm away.

I wish I didn't need glasses.

I wish my bangs would grow out.

I wish my bottom teeth weren't so crowded.

Inside Mom's bag, besides makeup, were floss, tweezers, Q-tips, an emery board, a pink plastic razor, lotion, and cologne. I was lining everything up on the counter when Matt started pounding on the door and shouting, "Stop hogging the bathroom!"

He is such a pain!

I considered spraying him with Mom's cologne or dotting the toilet seat with blue toothpaste blobs. But I just shouted back, "Hold your horses!"

Dad said, "C'mon, guys, let's go exploring!"

I felt like yelling, "I'm not a guy, and I *was* exploring!" But instead I put everything back and opened the door for Matt and said, "Your turn, Bratface."

Matt took one look at my face and said, "You look stupid."

I started rubbing off the makeup, but Mom said, "Let me fix you up, Sweet Pea." She reapplied the lipstick and gave me a French braid.

I thought I looked pretty good if I do say so myself.

Even Dad said I looked cute. Mom knows I'd rather look pretty than cute, but it was still nice of Dad to compliment me.

Anyway, we're about to go exploring.

Ready or not,

Melanie

bedtime 🛏️🕐 at the pensione

Dear Diary,

You know that tower Rapunzel was stuck in? Well, in Florence, or *Firenze* (Fee Ren Zay), there's this cool old palace bell tower that points up way above the other churches and buildings, and I can just picture Rapunzel inside it letting down her golden hair. In New York I bet that tower wouldn't even look tall. Old? Yup. Tall? Nope.

We crossed the *Ponte Vecchio* (Pon Tay Vecky Oh), or Old Bridge. It's so old that it was already old when Columbus discovered America! The bridge goes over the Arno River, and it has jewelry shops, ice cream stores, and scarf sellers right on it. Today was cloudy, so the Arno didn't look blue. It looked more like cappuccino and sort of matched the color of the buildings on its banks.

Here's the problem with Florence: the winding streets are too narrow for the traffic and crowds. We spent all day dodging cars, buses, mopeds, motorbikes, and motorcycles, trying not to get run over. At first Mom and Dad were holding hands (which they rarely do in New York), but soon Dad started cursing again (he said H-E-Double-Hockey-Sticks twice). He said city drivers are as crazy as highway drivers because they zoom around on motorbikes and don't wear helmets and park on sidewalks and yak on cell phones, and some even have kids riding behind them holding on for dear life.

"Motorbikes are dangerous," Mom agreed.

"Let's rent one," Matt said.

"What are you, mental?" I said.

Matt sang, "Twinkle, twinkle, little star, what you say is what you are."

We started arguing, but Dad told us to knock it off. I asked Dad why they built such little streets, and Dad explained that they didn't build them too narrow on purpose, they built them for people, horses, and carts, way before anyone thought about cars or buses.

31

"Or stretch limos," I added. "A stretch limo in Florence would get stuck for life."

Mom said, "Let's go to the *Uffizi*."

The *Uffizi* (Oo Feet Zee) is a big old museum that is supposed to be a "must-see." Mom and I waited on the longest longest longest line while Dad and Matt played catch nearby. Even Mom admitted she should have made a reservation, because some people got to cut in line.

Inside, Matt and I played a game he made up called Point Out the Naked People. We ran from painting to painting, and Mom didn't mind because at least we were paying attention to art.

She even took a turn. She pointed out a painting by Botticelli (Bah Ti Chelly) called *The Birth of Venus*. It shows this long-haired lady, the goddess of love and beauty, standing naked on a seashell. Matt said she looked like Barbie with no clothes on, but I said that Venus looked more like a *real* woman.

Mom also showed us a painting by Leonardo da Vinci (Lee Oh Nar Doe Duh Vin Chee). I thought it was lovely. Everyone is dressed, and the angel Gabriel is telling the Virgin Mary that she's pregnant. She wasn't even married to Joseph yet, but it was God's son, so it was a miracle.

I think Italy is full of miracles. I also think Italy is rated R.

Which I can handle. But maybe Mom and Dad should have left Matt at home with a baby-sitter.

Matt got hungry before I did. He said, "Dad, you said there are McDonald's all over Italy, and I want to go to one, and I'm putting my leg down."

I said, "Your foot, not your leg, dummy." But since I like McDonald's too, I started singing my latest poem:

Burger time, burger time,
I can make a burger rhyme.
Hand me a burger on a bun—
I will eat it 'til it's DONE!

Matt started singing along, but Mom and Dad said that instead of burgers we were going to buy bread, cheese, and salami and make a picnic. That was a good idea except that all the bread, cheese, and salami shops were *chiuso* (Q Zo), which means closed, which is what shops are in Italy at lunchtime. Restaurants stay open (duh), so even though we didn't go to McDonald's, we did find an outdoor *ristorante* (Ree Store On Tay) with lots of tables with umbrellas.

Dad and Mom ordered bean soup, and Matt and I ordered minestrone soup, and we all had *panini* (Pa Nee Nee), which means sandwiches. The ham in them was more dark pink than light pink, but I ate everything except for some bread, which I fed to the pigeons.

Pigeonwise, I was Miss Popularity. But as soon as they flocked around me, Matt scared them all away.

After lunch, Mom bought a pair of sunglasses and Dad looked at shoe stores and I checked out the postcard racks. Matt bought a stuffed balloon toy with a face drawn on it and yarn hair glued on top. It was like a squooshy Mr. Potato Head. First I told Matt that it was a dorky souvenir, but later I begged Mom to buy me one too. She did. So for a short while, we both had squooshy souvenirs.

At a little museum called the *Accademia* (Ack Ah Demmy Ya), Matt behaved inappropriately.

People from all over the world come to see this famous sculpture that Michelangelo (Michael Ann Jello) made almost five hundred years ago. It's of David, the guy in the Bible who, with stones and a slingshot, won a fight against a giant named Goliath.

What Michelangelo did was he took a huge hunk of marble and carved and carved until it looked like it could breathe. You can see the veins on David's hands, the nails on his toes, and all his shoulder muscles. David looks like one of those lifeguard guys who work out all the time.

Dad read in his guidebook that Michelangelo said, "David was already in the marble. I just took away everything that wasn't David."

Isn't that cool? When you think about it?

Mom said that when Michelangelo finished the *David*, everyone agreed it was a masterpiece except one important man. He thought the nose was too big. So Michelangelo took a handful of marble dust and a file and climbed a ladder in front of the man and tricked him by pretending to scrape away at the nose. He let some dust fall from his fingers, and the man said, "Ah! Now it's much better!" (Hee hee.)

Well, here's what I wanted to say: You can see David's you-know-what!

He's totally naked!!

Matt started pointing and giggling and taking his very last photos, so I giggled too. But Dad got mad and said, "Melanie, I thought you were more mature."

I hate when Dad says stuff like that.

I hate when Matt gets me in trouble.

He tried it again. When Dad wasn't looking, he pointed at David's behind and started laughing.

I told him to cut it out and that he would appreciate sculpture more when he grows up.

We walked down some more narrow streets, and suddenly there was the *Duomo* (Dwo Mo), this huge cathedral. In New York, St. Patrick's Cathedral is all one color: gray. The *Duomo* is covered with white, green, and pink marble. We climbed up the stairs inside, and then walked out and looked around at the red roofs of Florence. That was fun (for me, not my legs).

36

Dad took pictures, and Matt and I played catch with our squooshy things, but then I tossed mine to Matt, and Matt missed, so mine went *splat*, and the balloon ripped, and dusty white flour flew all over. Dad got mad at me, but it was Matt's fault. I told Matt to give me his squooshy thing, and he said, "No way." I lunged at him, but Mom stepped between us and told me to calm down this instant so we could all go out to dinner.

"McDonald's?" I asked.

Dad looked at me as if he couldn't believe he and I were even related. At least he couldn't send me to my room, since it's about a zillion miles away.

I made up a poem, so I said it out loud:

I am in an Awful mood.

Can we get some Chinese food ? ?

I thought the poem might make Mom and Dad at least smile, but Dad just said, "Melanie, we are on vacation, for heaven's sake. Stop being negative." Then he said I have the best problems of anyone he knows.

Which didn't exactly help me feel positive.

I looked at Matt, and he was smirking—the repulsive little newt.

Anyway, Mom and Dad took us to this fancy *ristorante*, and I thought things were about to improve. A jolly man welcomed us in and walked us past tables of yummy food—salami, melon, breads, pastries—and also some yucky stuff—roasted peppers, mushrooms, mussels, garlicky spinach. We sat down, and Mom and the man talked about what to order, and he kept saying that everything was *fantastico* (Fon Tos Teek Oh), which I figured meant fantastic. He didn't sound phony. He sounded like he loved everything on the menu. (He looked like he did too.)

Mmmm, mmmm, mmmm, I thought. *I can't wait.*

Well, I don't know what happened, but a few minutes later he was bringing out appetizers, and in front of me, he plunked a floppy pink baby octopus, grilled. It had eight disgusting tentacles and a million disgusting suckers. I was seriously GROSSED OUT.

More like horrified. I almost started to cry, but Dad quickly traded me his tortellini soup, and Mom started apologizing because she didn't know what the heck she had said that came out "octopus." (The special, maybe?)

For the main course, the man brought me spaghetti with meat sauce. But then he *immediately* ruined it by sprinkling parmesan cheese all over it. Mom and Dad both had sole as their main course, so I couldn't even trade.

Besides, this time no one even cared.

Matt, meanwhile, had pork chops with French fries, and was happy as can be. He called his French fries Italian fries, and Mom and Dad thought that was just so adorable. Like when he wants something and says, "Peas! Peas! Peas!" instead of "Please! Please! Please!" Or like once when Mom was going to take us to Central Park and Matt got all dressed up and Mom said, "Those are your best shoes!" and Matt said, "Those are my best feet too," and Mom just laughed.

Mom and Dad never stay mad at Matt.

After a while, Matt said, "I'm done. I can't eat any more." I couldn't either because I'd poked around and found enough unruined spaghetti.

Dad said, "Pass your plate over here."

Matt said, "It has my drool on it."

"Don't say 'drool,'" I told Matt. "Say 'saliva.'"

"Just pass the plate," Dad said, sounding mad again, and he ate up Matt's pork chops—drool and all—before paying the bill.

Mom asked, "Who wants *gelato*?" *Gelato* (Jay La Toe) means ice cream.

We all said, "Me! Me! Me!"

So we left and found an ice cream store under some streetlights, and Matt and I each got a cone. He bit off the bottom and started slurping out the ice cream. I felt like doing that too, but Dad was watching so I had to eat mine the regular way.

At least my cone lasted longer than Matt's.

We walked around, and I bought two more postcards. I could not, repeat *not*, buy a postcard of David standing there stark naked, so I bought a close-up of just his head. Even though Venus is acting more modest than David, she is every bit as butt naked, so I bought a postcard of just her head too.

Before we went back to our car, we stopped at the Straw Market to pet a bronze statue of a wild boar. They say that if you rub its snout, you will come back to Florence. Its snout is super shiny because everyone rubs it.

I rubbed it too. I do want to come back someday. But not with Matt the Brat. Or Dad the Grump. Maybe with Cecily. Or Christopher—on our honeymoon!

XOX, Melanie

P.S. My writing hand is now as tired as my walking feet.

Dear Diary,

I asked Mom and Dad if I could phone Cecily. They said, "Absolutely not," which I pretty much expected.

Cecily's middle name is Florence, and she dared me to ask my mother about girl things while we're in Italy. Actually, she double dared me. Cecily turned ten a while ago, and she thinks she's very mature. She grew out of her Barbies and gave them all to me. (Some were practically new, and others had really horrible haircuts.) Anyway, Cecily has been thinking about wearing a bra but is afraid to ask her mom. I'm not embarrassed to talk to my mother, but I'm also not developing! We're only in fourth grade!!

Speaking of bras, Italy is full of underwear stores and I figured out why.

Today Paola, the *pensione* lady, gave us toast and jam and juice and coffee and tourist tips. It was more like breakslow than breakfast, but we are now visiting fishing villages in *Cinque Terre* (Cheen Quay Tair Ay). The houses are pink and green and yellow, the streets are too narrow for cars, the boats bob up and down in the water, and the villages are all connected by trains.

I noticed clotheslines stretching along outside the windows. Dad said that most people in Italy hang their clothes out to dry because electricity is expensive. Well, if your panties were flapping in the wind, would you want your neighbors to see holes in them? I don't think so! Bad enough that people can see your underwear at all! I think that's why Italians need so much new underwear and so many underwear shops.

Mom says I'm very observant.

Once, in a garden, I observed two dragonflies mating.

Since Mom and I were on the subject of underwear, I asked, "Mom, when do you think I should wear a bra?"

"I don't know," Mom said. "It depends on when you need to and when you want to."

I said, "Okay," and that was that. I don't really get what the big deal is. Unless Cecily's mom doesn't want her to grow up or something.

My parents want me to grow up. Probably because

they still have Matt to be their itty-bitty cutesy-wutesy baby.

I want to grow up too, but I'm not in a mad rush. I mean, sometimes it's hard being the oldest kid in the family, because I'm not *that* old.

For example, Matt can laugh at naked statues, but I can't. Matt can eat ice cream cones from the bottom up, but I shouldn't. Matt can skip down the sidewalk to avoid stepping on cracks, but I'm supposed to walk like a young lady. Matt can hand Mom a gum wrapper, but when I try that, she says, "Hello? Do I look like a walking, talking trash can?" At the doctor's, Matt's eye chart has fun things like houses and apples, but mine has only plain letters. Even at McDonald's, Matt can ask for a Happy Meal, but Dad wants me to order just a burger for heaven's sake.

I wrote a new poem:

Fishing villages are quite quaint.
If I don't get lunch, I will
faint.

hungrily,
Melanie

Dear Diary,

After the train ride, we made sure to buy our picnic stuff while all the stores were still wide open. Well, at the cheese store there were about a billion different kinds of *formaggio* (For Ma Joe), and this woman behind the counter kept slicing tastes for me and Matt to try. She was smiling at us and sort of congratulating Mom and Dad for having *bambini bellissimi* (Bam Bee Nee Beh Lee See Me)—beautiful children—which was nice and all, except I'm much older than Matt, and she was acting as if we were six-year-old twins. Plus, she'd ask me, "*Ti piace?*" (Tee Pee Ya Chay), which means "Do you like it?" and I didn't have the heart to tell her that I'd have been a whole lot happier if she ran a candy store. Matt is pretty good at trying stuff, so he didn't have to fake-smile as much as I did.

Anyway, we took our picnic and walked on a footpath high up on the hillside above the blue blue sea. The path was called *Via dell'Amore* (Vee Ya Dell Ah More Ay), which means Lovers' Lane. I took two photos of

Mom and Dad. In one, they are kissing, and in the other, I told them to say, *"Formaggio!"*

When we got to an empty bench at the end of the path, we set up our picnic. Three flies buzzed over.

I sang, "Shoo, fly, don't bother me," but Matt acted all petrified.

"They're flies, not bees," I said.

"They have germs!" Matt said. "And look—is this fly poop?" He pointed to a teeny speck on his cheese.

"Oh, big whoop," I said. "Don't be such a baby."

"Eat your lunch," Mom said. "Flies don't poop."

"Yes they do, Mom," I said. "Everything poops. A fly would burst if it didn't poop."

"That's right," Matt agreed. "Even ticks and spiders poop. And when you had lice, Melanie, I bet they pooped all over your hair."

"You are so gross!" I said.

"In school," Matt said, "our goldfish sometimes swims around with a stringy poopy hanging from his tush."

"Not tush," Mom corrected. "Tail."

"Anus," I said.

"That is *enough!*" Dad said. "We're having a picnic,

and I do not want to hear any more talk about poop. Is that clear?"

"Matt started it," I said.

"I don't care *who* started it. I want it ended," Dad said.

Just then the sweetest little cat came by, and I took pictures and Matt fed it salami. Mom said cats love fishing villages because cats love fish. (Salami too, I guess.) Dad said Italy is shaped like a boot, so we could name the cat Puss in Boots.

I wanted to name it Little Ittle—the Ittle was for Italy. Matt wanted to name it Kitty.

I said, "That's a lame name." (Another rhyme!)

Matt hit me in the arm, so I hit him on the ear, and Dad glared at us and said, "Cut it out!"

Mom said, "Melanie, let's go buy a postcard." I knew she was just trying to change the subject. Well, we picked out a card, but Mom had credit cards and travelers' checks and zero Italian money, so Dad had to come over, and by the time we bought the postcard and Dad gave Mom some *lire* from his travel wallet, we realized that Matt had wandered off.

He was lost!

Mom and Dad both turned to me and asked, "Where's Matt?"

I said, "How am I supposed to know?"

At first I was mad at Matt for getting me in trouble again. But when we couldn't find him anywhere, I was worried. I mean, going up alone in our building elevator was one thing, but we're in a foreign country!

Dad went down to the docks to look for him, and Mom and I looked all around and climbed a stone tower and saw rooftops on one side and the sea on the other.

But no Matt.

I was getting *very* worried.

Finally, Mom said, "I bet he went looking for Little Ittle," so we went down an alleyway to a fish restaurant where we'd seen tons of cats.

And there he was! Petting a cat he had named

Pink Nose. Mom was relieved, but Dad yelled at Matt (hee hee), so I did too.

Matt said I was an E.B.S., which stands for Evil Big Sister.

I said he was an A.L.B., which stands for Annoying Little Brother. I even added, "You're so annoying, you're like a mosquito in human form."

Mom told us to stop fussing and asked, "Who wants *gelato*?"

We all said, "Me! Me! Me!"

In school, when we were studying families, Miss Sands said that oldest kids tend to be worriers and youngest kids tend to be spoiled. At least that's what I think she said. Doesn't that stink, though? If I had to pick between being worried or spoiled, I'd rather be spoiled.

Maybe I *am* spoiled, because after the ice cream, Mom and Dad bought us really cool Italian leather shoes. If I am spoiled, though, it's just the right amount.

On the drive back to our hotel, Matt felt carsick. Dad pulled over because, even though we were glad

Matt wasn't lost, we still didn't want him to puke his guts out all over our rented car.

Cars should have carsickness bags the way planes have airsickness bags.

We had to wait a while for Matt to feel better, so Mom pointed at the mountains and said, "Do you see those white streaks?"

Matt asked, "Is that snow?"

"Marble," Mom said. "Carrara (Car Rar Ah) marble." Mom said it's the kind that Michelangelo used for the *David*. She also said that even though David fought a giant, didn't David look like a giant himself?

I liked seeing how a mountainside could get turned into art. I also liked how David, who wasn't even a grown-up, was a giant because he saved the day.

I wish I could save the day and feel all proud of myself. Instead of getting blamed all the time.

Sincerely,

Melanie

afternoon at the pensione

Dear Diary,

You know what's worse than an air pocket? A pickpocket.

We went to Lucca (Loo Ca), which is a town surrounded by old stone walls that once protected it from bad guys. Dad parked the car just inside the walls, but he wasn't paying enough attention because he was about to see Puccini's house, and Puccini (Poo Chee Nee) wrote operas, and Dad loves opera.

I hate opera.

Dad says, "You'll like it when you're older."

I hate when he says that.

Anyway, Dad and Matt visited Puccini's house, and Mom and I went running in and out of churches that were cool and dark and churchy-smelling. Mom said they were "little jewels." I'm not that into churches, but I like being alone with Mom *without* Matt.

We had all agreed to meet on top of the Tower of Guinigi (Gwee Nee Gee), so Mom and I climbed up its bazillion stairs and got to the top, where there are actual oak trees growing. I'm not kidding. Big old shade trees sprouting up high above Lucca's red-tiled rooftops. It was so pretty and peaceful, I could have stayed forever. Of course, I had no clue about the Big Problems in store for us, and I also didn't think twice about the lavender-gray clouds right overhead. Well, by the time Dad and Matt arrived, Little Matt said he was keeling over from hunger, so that was that, we had to head straight down for lunch.

We ate in the *piazza* (Pee Ot Za). A *piazza* is a town square where people used to gather for meetings and to say hi and to buy and sell stuff. But this *piazza* was oval, not square, and it was mostly just full of restaurant tables and pigeons.

Matt felt underneath our table and said it had tons of A.B.C. gum stuck to it.

"A.B.C. gum?" Dad asked.

"Already Been Chewed," I explained.

"Wash your hands," Mom said. "Both of you."

We went to the bathroom, and I did not burn myself with the C-is-for-Hot water.

Matt gobbled his lunch in about two seconds, then started sneaking up on the pigeons to make them go flying. I like feeding them more than scaring them, but not Matt. He could spend all day chasing pigeons, just as Mom could spend all day looking at art.

I stayed seated. Dad told me to sit up straight and stop tipping my chair back. Mom said, "Napkin in your lapkin." Dad told me to use my fork, not my fingers. Mom told me to finish my pasta. I was tired of everyone telling me what to do and of watching Matt (since I didn't want him to get lost again), so after a while, I yawned in a really obvious I'm-getting-bored kind of way.

Dad asked, "What's wrong now?"

Without whining at all, I said, "You promised to take us to Pinocchio Park."

Dad ate his last bite of cannelloni and said, "You're right, kiddo. I did. Let's go."

But no one could remember where the car was!

Dad looked at his maps, and Mom asked people directions in her Italian, which must not be so great after all. (If it were *fantastico*, I wouldn't have been face-to-tentacles with an octopus the other night.) Well, the

Italians were pointing and waving and moving their hands around and smiling, but Mom just looked more and more confused. Then we walked ten minutes in one direction and ten in another, and still no car.

It's easier to get lost in Italy than in New York City. Why? Because at home it's mostly numbers (like Eighth Avenue and 16th Street) and straight streets that form a huge tic-tac-toe board. But here, instead of numbers, the streets have Italian names, and instead of being straight, they curve around and form a big fat maze.

The sky got darker, and the air got cooler.

It started to drizzle.

It started to rain.

It started to pour.

I wanted to take a taxi. That's what we do in New York. But Mom said, "Be patient." She and Dad weren't being patient.

Mom was saying, "Well, *think*, honey, where could it be?" And Dad was saying, "Sweetheart, you were there too. You tell me."

They were acting like Matt and me.

For fun, Matt and I decided to act like them. We all

got under this big awning, and Matt was saying, "I just love the opera. La la la la la!" and I was going in and out of invisible churches and saying, "Oh, what a little jewel!" Then Matt said, "This is excellent wine," so I said, "Napkin in your lapkin, Melanie." Then Matt said, "The car is this way!" so I said, "No, no, it's *this* way!"

Instead of laughing, Dad threatened to give us a time-out.

I'm a little old for a time-out.

Sometimes I'd like to give Dad a time-out.

Matt said, "I wish it wasn't raining water."

I said, "What do you want it to rain?"

"Lemonade."

"That would make everything sticky."

"Milkshakes."

"That would make everything gloppy."

"Hot chocolate."

"That would burn people."

"M&M's."

I agreed that M&M's would be good, but I said they would hurt if they hit you. Matt said everybody could use upside-down umbrellas called candy-catchers.

He's obviously been thinking about this.

I couldn't decide if Matt was being cute or dumb or if he'd just gone loco in Lucca. But then I noticed two guys standing next to Dad, helping him find where we were on the map. One started leaning in really close to Dad. Too close! One of his hands was on the map, but the other was reaching toward Dad's pants pocket! Right when I figured out what was going on, the man grabbed Dad's travel wallet, and both guys ran. *Zoom!* Through the rain and around the corner. Dad was about to run after them, but Mom wouldn't let him.

I wish I could have warned Dad and saved the day.

Dad blamed himself for being such an "easy target"—such an obvious tourist, with his guidebook in his hand and his camera around his neck. He said he had had about 150 dollars in Italian money, which was now gone gone gone. He had had credit cards too, but at least he could call a phone number to cancel them. He also had had a photo of me holding Matt when he was a baby, and he hated to lose that, and the thieves wouldn't even want it.

Dad felt terrible. Since he was so mad at himself,

Mom stopped being mad at him, so that was one good thing. But then Matt started crying. I think it worried him to see that even parents do stupid stuff. Plus, he had been playing catch with his squooshy toy and he dropped it in a puddle and the flour made a gloppy mess—so no more souvenir.

Well, we found a police station and made a bunch of phone calls, and a policeman wrote down everything Mom said. It took forever, and at the end, he said we should be more careful.

Duh. Thanks a lot, Officer.

Personally, if I were my parents, I would have felt pretty embarrassed to have to admit that we got pickpocketed and that oh, by the way, we had no idea where our car was. I mean, I doubt the policeman was impressed with how smart we were. He took us to a bank machine so we could get more money, and Mom let me press the buttons. It was cool how colorful Italian *lire* came shooting out instead of old green American dollars.

Fortunately, the policeman drove us around until we found our car. And Mom and Dad stopped arguing. And

Mom still has our passports and a different credit card. And we're all together. At home, Dad's always away on business and Mom has meetings meetings meetings.

Since it stopped raining and the day wasn't over, we did go to Collodi to see Pinocchio Park. It has long, skinny metal sculptures of Pinocchio, Geppetto, and Jiminy Cricket. Matt and I sat next to some Italian children at a puppet theater. We understood about Pinocchio's nose and everything, but we didn't really get all the jokes since they were in Italian. Well, every time the Italian children laughed their heads off, Matt laughed his head off too, ho ho ho ho ho, just like Santa Claus.

"Why are you laughing? You don't even get it," I said, but he kept laughing like a little hyena.

Somehow he made friends with an Italian boy his age, and they slid on slides together and played inside the jaws of Monstro, the whale that almost ate up Pinocchio.

I didn't see anyone my age to hang out with. Even if I had, I probably would have been too embarrassed to say *ciao* (Chow), which can mean both hi and bye. I was looking at an Italian dad pushing his son on a swing, and an Italian mom walking with her teenage daughter holding the crook of her arm, and Mom and Dad talking on a bench, and Matt playing with his new friend. Suddenly I felt a little homesick, which was strange considering I was with my entire family.

I started wondering if the four of us stick out more than we blend in. Dad had on his palm-tree vacation shirt with jeans and sneakers, but Italian men, I noticed, wear more formal clothes and loafers. Mom also had on jeans and sneakers, whereas Italian women look all stylish, as if they could be heading off to church or a party. And Matt, in his baggy T-shirt and sweatpants, was a total ragamuffin next to his Italian buddy in khakis.

I was beginning to feel self-conscious about my own pants and top too. I mean, some Italian teenage girls wear their jeans so tight, I don't know how they even wriggle into them. And they don't wear them with regular long-sleeved shirts and sneakers but with body-hugging sweaters and high-heeled sandals. If we ever moved to Italy, I bet it would take me months just to figure out how to dress right.

Anyway, my favorite part of Pinocchio Park was when we left, because you have to exit through the gift shop. There is absolutely no other way out. Mom and Dad didn't like that. Matt and I did. He bought an ornament thingy that if you pull a string, Pinocchio's arms and legs go up. I bought postcards—because, after all, Pinocchio is not naked!

The reason there's a park, or *parco* (Par Co), about Pinocchio in Collodi is that the author of the book that became the movie that became the video liked the town so much that when he finished writing, instead of signing his name, he signed Collodi.

Mom said creative people sometimes use different names. Mark Twain and Marilyn Monroe and Ringo Starr and Dr. Seuss are all made-up names.

Maybe I should call myself *Melanie the Magnificent*

Or spell Melanie without the e. Or keep the e but dot the i with a flower or a heart.

Or maybe instead of worrying about how I will

someday sign my work, I should worry about doing my Romework homework—writing that stupid thirty-line poem. It's starting to hang over my head like another lavender-gray rain cloud.

forever yours,
Melani

bedtime 🛏️🕐 at the pensione

Dear Diary,

I wanted us to go out for dinner, but Mom and Dad said that it was our last night at the *pensione*, and Paola wanted to make a farewell dinner, and they had already paid for it. Not only that, but Paola asked Mom if I would help cook it with her, and Mom said yes—without even consulting me.

Next thing you know, Paola and I were in her kitchen, wearing aprons, up to our elbows in a gooey mixture of flour, water, and yeast. She didn't use a cookbook, measuring cup, mixer, spoon, or anything. She just tossed a bunch of ingredients on a board and let me help squoosh and squash and squeeze the dough.

While we waited for the dough to rise, we opened a big jar of tomatoes and cooked up tomato sauce. Paola added a little garlic and a tiny bit of basil, but she could tell by my face that I like my sauce *plain*—with no thingamajigs. We also grated a big ball of mozzarella cheese.

Once our dough doubled in size, we stretched and pulled and pinched it, then rolled it into four flat circles.

We went outside to light up Paola's stone-and-brick oven, which is heated by burning wood. It looks like a fireplace with a chimney but no house. Then we spread the tomato sauce and cheese on the dough.

TA! DA! PIZZA!

We put the pizzas on a tray attached to a long wooden pole. Next we put the tray in the hot oven and tilted it so the pizzas slid off. The pizzas rose and bubbled and got all golden. Since Paola couldn't speak English and I couldn't speak Italian, we just pointed and smiled a lot, and then she showed me how to slide the tray back under the pizzas to yank them out.

I must confess, it was pretty cool. I've made frozen pizza before, and I've put tomato sauce and mozzarella on bagels, but I've never ever made homemade pizza from scratch.

Well, we all had dinner together, and everyone said, *"Grazie"* (Grot See Yay) to Paola and, "Thank you" to me. We ate up all four pizzas—including the crusts, or as Matt says, the pizza bones. Matt said it was the best pizza and the best pizza bones he ever ate.

Happily yours,

*Chef
Melani*

March 24
in the Car

Dear Diary,

Matt left teeth marks on my thigh for no reason, and no one even cares. It's so not fair! If I ever bit him, I'd probably be thrown in jail.

We packed our stuff, hugged Paola good-bye, and are driving south to Rome. I said that it was our fifth day in Italy and I still didn't know what to write about for my poem. Matt said I was being a big crybaby about it.

I might have complained a few times, but I never once cried. He's the one who was boohooing away yesterday.

Matt said, "Why are you so worried? You like to write. What do you think is in your diary? Pictures?"

I said, "It could be a sketchbook. How would you even know, Butthead?"

"Because I read it."

"Did not."

"Did too."

"You can hardly even read."

"Can so. I read it this morning when you were taking a bath."

"Did not."

"Did too. I read that you called me Matt the Brat."

"I'm going to kill you!" I said. "You *are* a brat, and I hate your guts."

That's when Matt bit me. Right in the car. I'm surprised there wasn't blood splashing all over the place.

And did Mom and Dad yell at him? No. Dad told us both to pipe down so we wouldn't have an accident. Then Mom took Matt's side and scolded me! Me!!

I couldn't believe it! I'm guilty until proven innocent! And Dad is supposed to be a lawyer!

He said he expects better behavior from both of us if we ever want to go on another family trip.

Which I sort of do.

Either that, or open a store with a sign that says Little Brothers for Sale.

But who would want to buy a little brother?

I've decided not to say another word for the rest of the vacation. Not one.

That will make them sorry.

But what I *feel* like saying is that there is too much pressure on me to write a poem and take care of Matt and keep track of the car and look out for pickpockets and make sure nothing bad ever happens.

We've been driving driving driving. Most of the other cars have white oval stickers with a big black I for *Italia* (Ee Tal Ya) on them. Usually by now Matt and I would have started a game of Sweet & Sour. That's when we smile and wave at other drivers and try to make them smile and wave back. If they do, they're sweet. If they don't, they're sour. But we're not playing because I'm not talking.

Mom is. She keeps telling us to look at the "light on the landscape" and the "golden glow of the distant towers" and the "silver leaves of the olive trees." It's like she's in love or something.

Well, I am looking. Just not talking.

Dad said that we needed some gas, so Matt said, "I have gas!" and blew on his arm to make farty noises. He's trying to get me to laugh but I won't. Dad said to Matt, "Keep it down in the rear," but Matt said, "The rear?" and started cackling and snorting even more.

Not me. I am still—

silently yours,

MAD MEL

afternoon in our hotel in Rome)

Dear Diary,

We drove and drove, and little by little the olive groves and apricot trees and rosemary bushes turned into road signs and highways and shopping areas.

Rome is huge: like Manhattan, except that Manhattan is an island surrounded by water, whereas Rome has a river curving right through it. Also, Rome is much older than New York. It could be New York's great-great-great-great-great-great-great-great-great-grandfather. At least!

We checked into our new hotel, and Mom and Dad let us order from room service. I love room service. I love this hotel, even though I'll bet that nobody here is as nice as Paola.

Matt and I have our own room and bathroom, and Mom and Dad have their own room and bathroom. A door connects our two rooms.

Outside our window, we can see a bridge over the Tiber River and lots of people and cars rushing across it to get to whatever side they are not on.

After lunch, Mom and Dad closed their door because they wanted to take a nap, and Matt was listening to a tape, so I worked hard on my poem because I want to get it done. This is what I've written so far:

> The cats are all cute
> In Italy's boot.
>
> I liked the pizza and Uffizi,
> But waiting on line was not too easy.
>
> I liked Lucca's old stone walls.
> I hope Pisa's tower never falls.
>
> I learned a few Italian words.
> Matt learned to chase Italian birds.

I was really happy, and I copied it over neatly.

I even decided to start talking again, so I read my poem to Matt.

That was a BIG mistake. Not counting that last line about him, which he loved, he said the same thing he said last time.

He said it was stupid.

So I said the same thing I said last time.

I said he was stupid.

We started fighting, and that woke up Mom and Dad, and they came in and got mad at us. I told them I wanted to read them my poem.

Dad said, "Not now."

He could have said, "Yippee! Melanie is talking again!" but I don't think he even noticed I'd been giving them the silent treatment.

If Matt had stopped talking, he would have noticed.

Mom said we were going to the *Villa Borghese* (Vee La Bor Gay Zay) park and that first we all had to go to the bathroom.

Well, this is sort of gross, but whenever Mom says to go to the bathroom, I rush to go first. Why? Because when Matt goes, he either puts the seat up and forgets to put it down YUCK, or he doesn't put the seat up and he gets sprinkles of pee right on the seat double yuck!

Mom and Dad just don't understand how hard it is to have a little brother, because they never had one.

Very truly yours,

EVEN MADDER MEL!

Dear Diary,

The Villa Borghese was a giant *parco* full of couples, families, strollers, sunbathers, joggers, Rollerbladers, bikers, and people throwing sticks to their dogs. We rented bicycles and peddled all over the place. It was the first time we ever went bicycling as a family. I got my own bicycle, and I kept up with Mom and Dad, no problem. Matt was too young to get his own bike (ha ha), so he sat behind Dad and held on tight.

I know it sounds unsafe, especially since nobody in the park was wearing a helmet and neither were we. But that's how it is here, and as Dad said, "When in Rome, do as the Romans do."

In Florence, Dad was all worked up about safety, but today he was acting like it was no big deal. (Parents can be hard to figure out!)

Well, guess who ended up falling?

Hint: Not Matt.

Me! I tried to swerve out of the way of a bunch of teenagers, and down I went. Not on my head—on my butt! It was pretty embarrassing. But the teenagers didn't laugh; they helped me up (which made it even more embarrassing).

After we returned the bikes, Mom wanted to go to another museum, but we said no. I wanted to eat Chinese food, but everyone said no. Matt suggested we eat spaghetti, and of course Mom and Dad said sure. So we did. Dad ordered his *al dente* (Al Den Tay), which means more chewy than soft. He says that even in English, people use that expression.

I've never heard it.

Here's the bad thing that happened. Matt just realized that he left DogDog at the *pensione*. So now Matt is in bed next to me, sniffling pitifully. Mom and Dad said they would call Paola and ask her to send DogDog to this hotel. I hope they do, because Matt says he can't sleep without DogDog to guard him. I considered saying, "I'll guard you," but I didn't feel like it.

Buona notte,
Mellie

71

Dear Diary,

We walked our feet off today. Right now we're on top of this high hill that we hiked up so we could watch the sun set over Rome, the capital of Italy. Julius Caesar and Cleopatra used to have dates around here.

I like having all of Rome at my feet. I've been up the Empire State Building, and it's cool because you're surrounded by other skyscrapers. But what I like about this view is that you're outside the city, so you can sort of take it all in. I mean, Rome has been growing and action-packed for, well, almost forever. Rome was here before people even knew about TV or cars or freezers or Scotch tape or e-mail or vaccines or M&M's or anything.

Dad said Rome is called the Eternal City.

Mom pointed out the Vatican and said that tomorrow we'll see the Sistine Chapel—"one of the masterpieces of the world."

It took Michelangelo almost five years to paint

the whole ceiling, and he had to do it lying down on a bunch of scaffolding with paint dripping on him from above, and he didn't even like to paint as much as he liked to sculpt.

"Did the paint drip into his ears and nostrils?" Matt asked.

"Probably," Mom said, looking sort of sad for Michelangelo. She told us that one reason why Michelangelo sculpted so well was because he had done something illegal.

"Against the law?" Matt asked, his eyes all big and round.

"Against the law of the time," Mom said. "He dissected corpses so he could better understand human anatomy."

"Huh?" Matt said.

"He cut up dead people," Mom explained, "so he could see how their muscles and bones hung together."

Matt didn't say another word. Michelangelo is a lot to think about.

This morning Mom asked, "Who remembers the *David?*"

Dad and Matt and I all said, "Me! Me! Me!" because it's fun to say "Me! Me! Me!"

So Mom said, "Let's go see two more of his marble sculptures," and we followed her around like a bunch of art students from one big musty church to another.

The first sculpture was of Moses carrying the Ten Commandments. Moses has funny little horns popping out of his head. Mom said they symbolize rays of light.

The second sculpture was of Jesus carrying the cross. After Michelangelo made it, some religious people thought it was inappropriate to see Jesus' you-know-what, so they added a big bronze loincloth.

Matt said, "It looks like a metal diaper."

Mom agreed they should not have changed his work: "You don't tamper with genius."

We also walked around and took photos of this big old column and visited a place called Trajan's Market, which used to be a giant shopping center like an ancient A&P or Zabar's, but now it's just mounds of red bricks piled up on each other. Lots of stray cats and kittens seemed curious about us, but they wouldn't let us get too close. (I wish we'd brought salami!) Dad told us to forget the cats and try to picture people from biblical times bustling around and buying oil and spices.

Matt said he was a "Starvin' Marvin" and he didn't want to picture dead people buying food, he wanted to eat food. So we went into the nearest pizzeria and ordered lunch. While we were waiting, I figured it would be an excellent time to show Mom and Dad my poem.

I took it out of my pocket. It was a little wrinkled, but I started reading it out loud, all eight lines.

When I was halfway done, Matt took his gum out of his mouth and put it on the tip of his knife and held it over the candle on our table as if he were toasting a marshmallow.

Dad told him to behave.

I kept on reading my poem, and when I finished, I was sure everybody would compliment me.

But Matt put his finger down his throat as though he were about to throw up, and Mom scolded him but didn't say one word to me.

Finally Dad said, "It's cute," then made about a million suggestions.

I was hoping Mom would defend me and say, "You don't tamper with genius."

But she didn't. She just agreed that my poem was cute.

"This poem is not supposed to be cute! I worked hard on it!"

"Simmer down," Dad said. "No one expects you to be Dante."

"Who's Dante?" I asked.

"A famous Italian poet," Mom said.

"You didn't work that hard on it," Matt said. "You whipped it off because you wanted to get it over with."

"You don't get it!" I said. "I hate you!" I couldn't believe I said "I hate you!" right at lunch.

Dad said, "Don't talk that way, young lady."

"It's okay," Matt said. "I'm used to it."

"Melanie, I know you're angry," Mom said, "but apologize to your brother."

I mumbled, "Sorry," but I felt like kicking him under the table. Or pushing his tiny heinie right off his chair.

Mom said, "You're off to a good start with your poem. I'm sure you can do even better."

"I agree," Matt said. Little turd.

"Rome wasn't built in a day," Dad added. "More like a couple thousand years."

Lunch came, and Matt grabbed a big slice of pizza and ate it right up, and no one even realized that I was still mad.

Which I was.

Or maybe Mom did realize it, because after a while she put a slice in front of me.

I was going to let it sit there and get cold, but Dad said,

> Melanie, *dear, you've written quite wittily.*
> Now eat your pizza and let's enjoy Italy.

Mom laughed, and you could tell Dad thought he was the poet of the world.

I didn't feel like pizza. I felt like punching someone's guts out.

Matt's, for instance.

D curse D curse D curse,
MELANIE

P.S. The sun is now setting and Rome looks all rosy, and you can sure tell that it wasn't built in a day.

bedtime 🕐🚌 at the hotel

Dear Diary,

Matt is still upset because DogDog isn't back, even though Paola promised to send him. To cheer Matt up, I started playing circus and doing acrobatics on the hotel bed with him. I was getting really good until by mistake I flipped upside down in the air and landed on the floor on my face. My eyebrow rammed into the frame of my glasses, and my glasses didn't break, but my eyebrow got a gash in it and was all bloody.

Mom and Dad came in, and I could tell Mom was trying not to get hysterical. She kept saying, "At least your eye is okay. At least your eye is okay."

Dad said he would stay with Matt, and Mom should take me to the hospital since she speaks Italian. Dad sort of rocked me on his lap and held a cold wet washcloth to my eye while Mom called down to the front desk of the hotel and told them to have a taxi ready.

Next thing you know, Mom and I were in the emergency room.

Mom started babbling away in Italian, and after a

long wait, with me sitting between a wheezing old man and a lady with a broken finger, the receptionist said it was my turn. A nurse gave me a lollipop, and a handsome young Italian doctor said in English, "I am plastic surgeon. I help you." He had a little accent, and he said, "You are pretty girl—I will make sure you remain pretty girl." (That was sweet.)

He gave me three shots right in my eyebrow to make it totally numb, and then he said, "This won't hurt" and sewed seven tiny stitches. I've never had stitches before, but I didn't feel them. (Phew.)

I was almost glad I didn't speak Italian because I didn't want to have to explain to the handsome young doctor about pretending to be an acrobat.

I did thank him in Italian, though. I said, "*Grazie.*"

Back at the hotel, Dad said he couldn't believe what a good job the doctor did. He said I looked cute as ever. I thought Matt might say I looked like Frankenstein because of the stitches, but Matt didn't say anything, he just hugged me. Mom said we were lucky a plastic surgeon was available.

Cecily once told me that plastic surgeons are the

doctors who give old ladies face-lifts to get rid of their wrinkles and who give big fake Barbie bosoms to ladies who want them. I think it's weird to have surgery if you don't need to, but I'm glad plastic surgeons are also the doctors who repair kids who've been in accidents.

Mom and Dad made us promise not to do any more acrobatics in Italy.

Duh.

ALL STITCHED UP,
MELANIE

P.S. Here's how to say eyebrow in Italian: *Sopracciglio* (So Pra Cheel Yo).

March 26
afternoon

on a 🚃 in the Sistine Chapel

Dear Diary,

Matt is lost. Really and truly and forever lost this time.

And it's my fault.

Mom and Dad would probably kill me, except then they would have no children at all.

Also we're in the Vatican, which is where the Pope lives, so it's not exactly an ideal place to kill your kid. Mom and Dad are freaking out because Matt has completely totally utterly absolutely 100 percent disappeared. They said they can find him faster without me. They also said I'm old enough to be alone and to keep an eye out for Matt myself.

I wanted to argue, but Mom was getting hysterical again.

Poor Mom.
Poor Matt.
Poor ME!

I'm sitting in the Sistine Chapel, being good as gold, not moving an inch. Mom and Dad said to STAY PUT and SIT STILL and DON'T GO ANY-WHERE. Mom gave me her whole lecture about how if some stranger says, "Come and help me find my lost kitten," or "Come with me and I'll give you candy," that I should say, "NO." I didn't say, "Duh," or "I'm not five, Mom." I just nodded. Then Mom taught me the Italian word for "help," which is *aiuto* (Eye Oo Toe). And she said not to be scared.

That's when I started getting scared.

I mean, I may be double digits, but it's not like I'm a teenager or anything.

Anyhow, I'm sitting on this bench, behaving, not moving an inch, just staring at Michelangelo's ceiling and looking for Matt and making little bets with myself, like: If I write one more page in my diary, Matt will suddenly come back.

So far he hasn't.

I'm not religious, but I keep staring up at God creating heaven and earth, and God giving life to Adam, and God creating Eve, and Adam and Eve getting kicked out of the Garden of Eden.

And I keep wondering if God is staring back at me.

I also wonder if it would help if I prayed. And if I promised to be nicer to Matt or something.

I'm worried worried worried.

Matt can be an A.L.B., but I still wish he would pop up and say, "Boo!"

The reason it's my fault is that I wished Matt would get lost. I wished it. I did.

Early this morning we went to the Trevi Fountain, which has sculptures of men and horses and even of Neptune (who looks like King Triton in *The Little Mermaid* movie I used to like). Everyone was making wishes and throwing coins into the fountain. Mom and Dad threw Italian coins over their shoulders and gave me an American penny and Matt an American dime.

Dimes are small, but since they're worth ten times more than pennies, I said, "That's not fair!" I doubt Matt even knows that dimes are more valuable, so he wouldn't have cared what Mom and Dad gave him. He was so busy scaring pigeons, he probably wouldn't have cared if Mom and Dad hadn't given him any money.

Dad said, "What does it matter, Melanie? You're not spending it. You're throwing it. Quit whining."

Mom said, "All the coins go to the Red Cross anyway—just make a wish and toss it in."

You'd think they would be nicer to me now that I'm wounded.

Well, even though I was still mad about the dumb penny, I did start thinking about what to wish. That Mom and Dad would let me have a slumber party? That Christopher would like me back (or at least be aware of my existence)? While I was thinking, Matt came hopping over on one foot and waved his shiny little dime at me like a big show-off and stuck out his little snake tongue. So I wished I never even had a brother.

And now I don't.

The other reason why it's my fault is that Matt and I got into another big fat fight, and I was really mean to him. At the time, I thought he deserved it. Mom and Dad took us to St. Peter's, which Dad said is in *The Guinness Book of Records* because it's the world's largest church, topped by the world's largest dome.

It *is* huge.

Inside, behind thick glass, is the *Pietà* (Pee Yay Tah), which Michelangelo sculpted when he was very young. It shows Mary holding Jesus after he died. Mary looks so so so sad.

Matt was asking why it has glass in front of it, and Dad said that in 1972 some loony person damaged the Madonna's head with a hammer, and they fixed it, but now they want to protect it with the glass shield.

Matt said, "I don't get it."

I said, "Get what?"

He opened his eyes wide, then scrunched up his face, which made his freckles sort of mush together, and asked, "Madonna's here?"

I said, "Is *your* head damaged, Freckle Face? Not Madonna the singer. Madonna the Virgin Mary. You can be so *stupido*" (Stoo Pee Doe). That's Italian for stupid.

Matt said, "Stop picking on me."

I said, "Stop being *stupido*."

He pinched me.

I said, "Get lost."

And this is the terrible part: He did.

Dad came back. I was right where he left me. "Have you seen him?" he asked.

I shook my head and felt like I was going to cry.

It almost seemed like Dad might cry too. He said, "Stay right here. We'll be back. We'll find him."

He gave me a hug and said not to worry.

Then he left, and I kept worrying.

Besides having stitches in my eyebrow, I have tears in my eyes and a lump in my throat.

I don't want to cry, though. Or look obvious. I don't want some stranger asking me if *I'm* lost.

Every time I look up, I have to blink a bunch of times or the ceiling gets blurry. I keep staring at the part of the painting where God's hand almost touches Adam's, and I wish wish wish more than anything that I had never let go of Matt's hand.

What happened was that when we got on line to see the Sistine Chapel, it was so crowded that Mom and Dad held hands and told us to hold hands too.

Which we were doing.

We went through the Candelabra Gallery, the Tapestry Gallery, the Map Gallery, the Raphael Rooms, and about a million other rooms because Mom wanted to take the long way. I was holding Matt's hand the whole entire time.

Finally, we got to the Sistine Chapel. It is a "must-see." Dad had his nose in his guidebook, and Mom had her eyes on the ceiling, and I figured we were where we had to be. So I let go of Matt's hand.

It truly is my fault.

Mom just came back in to check on me. I haven't budged from my spot on the bench.

"No Matt?" she asked.

I started to cry. Actually, sob. People were staring and it was embarrassing, but I couldn't help it. "Mom," I said, "I let go of his hand."

"It's not your fault, Sweet Pea. We're going to find him."

"It *is* my fault," I said, even though I didn't tell her about my wish at the fountain.

"It's not your fault. Matt is your brother, not your responsibility." I was glad she said that. Dad had made it sound like he was my brother *and* my responsibility. "You're not supposed to take care of the family—we're supposed to take care of you," Mom said. "And listen. We're going to find Matt. I just talked to a policeman."

Another policeman! We are troublemaker tourists. That policeman in Lucca told us to be more careful, and we were *less* careful!

Mom held my hand and I didn't let go. But then she said she had to keep looking, so I had to let go.

This room is jam-packed with people—I keep wishing one would be Matt!

Instead of the ceiling, I've started looking at the wall. Mom told me that when Michelangelo was an old man, he spent another five years painting the wall of the Sistine Chapel. The wall painting is called *The Last Judgment*, and it shows Jesus after he came back to Earth. He has little holes in his hands and feet where the nails were when he was on the cross. He is surrounded by hundreds of naked dead people sort of swirling around him. Jesus is sending the bad ones to h—ll and the good ones to heaven. Most of the people look scared and miserable.

I don't know if I'm a good person or a bad person, but I do know that I am scared and miserable.

I wish Matt would come back.

I wish Mom and Dad would come back too. I can't go looking for them, because they told me to STAY PUT.

So here I am, parked on the bench, with God above keeping me company.

worried,
Mel

Dear Diary,

THEY FOUNd MATT ! HURRAY !

I looked up at God and sort of mumbled, "*Grazie*."

I guess lots of policemen in the Vatican got on their walkie-talkies and cell phones and started looking for a six-year-old *americano* (Ah Mare Ee Con Oh) with freckles and a striped shirt and sneakers with Velcro instead of laces. I mean, a lost kid is a bigger deal than a pickpocketed wallet.

It turns out that Matt had wandered back to the Map Gallery and was slumped under an ancient map of Italy.

He said he was going to talk to a guard, but he was too scared.

We all hugged, and Matt was crying, and I reached into my pocket and gave him my very last piece of American gum. New, not A.B.C.

Dad said, "Let's get out of here."

91

Mom said, "Who wants *gelato?*"

Guess what we said.

same day

bedtime at the hotel

Dear Diary,

Matt made me promise not to tell, but I don't think it counts as breaking the promise if I tell you.

He got lost on purpose!

(He didn't mean to get so so so lost.)

When he first told me, I was about to say, "Well, that was stupid!" but I'm glad I didn't, because he said he stomped off because Mom and Dad weren't paying attention to him and I was always calling him stupid.

I was going to say, "Oh, so now it's mmmyyyy fault?"

but instead I said, "I just call you stupid because you're my little brother. All fourth graders call their little brothers stupid."

"Well, it hurts my feelings," he said. "And I don't like when you call me Matt the Brat either."

I was going to say, "What should I call you? Matt the Gnat?" but instead I told him that I said nice things about him in my diary too. Which is a tiny bit true.

"Yeah, right." I could tell he didn't believe me.

"I do."

"Prove it."

I showed him where I wrote, "Matt can be pretty cute sometimes." (I covered up where I wrote, "Or dumb. It depends on my mood.")

"See?" I said.

"Even in school some kids are mean to me."

"Like who?"

"Like Kurt. He laughs at me just like you do. Once I fell in the playground, and he laughed so hard I wanted to kick him, but I couldn't because the principal was there."

"Oh, Matt," I said, "You're a good kid. You're just a brat sometimes." I even put my arm around him.

I don't know who was more surprised—me or Matt.

"You're a brat sometimes too," he said, and looked at me with his blue eyes and long lashes.

For some reason we both laughed. I mean, Matt can annoy me and worry me, but I wouldn't really trade him in.

"Kurt is a twerpy pea-brain," I said. "You don't like him, so who cares if he doesn't like you?" I was mad at Kurt for being mean to Matt, and I was proud of myself for not being an E.B.S. "When someone says something mean, let it be like a ball that bounces off you instead of like gum that sticks to you," I said, sounding like Mom. Matt sort of nodded. "What matters," I said, "is what your friends think of you."

"My friends like me."

"There you go," I said. "Like Luke and Lily."

"Especially Lily," Matt said, and smiled.

"Especially Lily," I repeated. "Want me to give you a postcard to send her?"

"Okay," Matt said.

If I don't watch out, I'm going to get the P.B.S. award for Perfect Big Sister.

Then I'll get on P.B.S. with Bert and Barney. (Get it? P.B.S.?)

Matt and I both think Barney is *stupido*. So I started singing that song you can't get out of your head, and Matt joined in:

> *I hate you,*
> *You hate me,*
> *We're a stupid family*
> *With a bang! bang! bang!*
> *Barney's on the floor—*
> *No more purple dinosaur.*

I'm about to turn off the lights in Matt's and my room. I'm also about to say to him, "Don't ever get lost again."

That'll be pretty mushy—for me.

Love
Melani the P.B.S.

Dear Diary,

I went to the bathroom and fell in because Stupid Matt left the stupid seat up. I was going to wake him and yell at him, but he's fast asleep, his mouth flopped open like a fish, and he still doesn't have DogDog. So I'm leaving him alone. This time.

M.

March 27

morning in the hotel.

Dear Diary,

DogDog is back. Matt is happy as can be. A bellhop delivered DogDog in a package, and Matt is holding him so tightly that if he were a real dog, he'd be dead as a doornail.

I don't know how old the bellhop was, but he didn't seem very old at all. He was tall and cute, with brown eyes and hair that was sort of messy, as though he'd just rubbed it with a balloon. He seemed friendly, so I decided to try out my Italian words on him. First I said, *"Fantastico!"* and *"Grazie!"*

He smiled and said, *"Prego"* (Pray Go), which means "You're welcome." Then he said, *"Parli italiano?"* (Par Lee Ee Tal Ya No), which means "Do you speak Italian?"

So I said, *"Un po,'"* (Oon Poe), which means "A little."

Then he said, *"Sei americana?"*

Well, that sounded like "Say 'Americana,'" so I said, "Americana."

He laughed and pointed to me and said, *"Americana?"*

I smiled and said, *"Si"* (See) and added, "New York."

Then I copied his question and asked, *"Sei italiano?"*

Well, duh duh duh, obviously he was Italian, but I couldn't think of anything else I knew how to say!

He said, *"Sono romano,"* which I figured meant he was from Rome. Then he stuck out his hand and said, "Giorgio," so I stuck out mine and said, "Melanie," and we shook hands. I was sort of smiling and blushing, and then he said, *"Ciao"* to both Matt and me.

I like how *ciao* means both hi and bye. I hope I'll get to say hi and bye to Giorgio again.

When I closed the door, Matt was still hugging Dog-Dog, so I started hugging Hedgehog.

But here's the weird thing. There was something about Giorgio that seemed really familiar, but I couldn't figure out what. Then suddenly it dawned on me.

Giorgio was tall and brown-eyed with stick-uppy hair—like Norbert!

Could that mean I think Norbert is cute?

I don't think so!

But you know what? I will say that as far as dorks go, Norbert is a decent dork. And I don't really *hate* him. After all, he did help me in the cafeteria with my runaway potato. And so what if his shirts are a little bright? It takes time to figure out what clothes people consider normal. As for his accent, the plastic surgeon had an accent in English, and I must have an accent in Italian, and if you say, "Tennis shoes ten issues tennis shoes ten issues," I guess they really do sound about the same. (I've been thinking about pronunciation ever since we got here. It's complicated! Pizza is an Italian word we say in English, but how do we say it?

"Pete Sa" or "Pete's Za"? There's not always only one right way.)

While I'm writing about Norbert, of all people, I might as well add that although I don't think picking your nose is a wonderful hobby, it's not like I've never ever ever ever done it. I just would never do it in school. And maybe Norbert never did either. Cecily doesn't know *everything*.

When she had a Valentine's Day party, her mom made her invite the whole class, and Cecily sent Norbert's invitation a week after everyone else's. When she told me, I laughed. But now I think that just because he's a little geeky doesn't mean that people should be mean to him. I know Cecily is popular and Norbert isn't, but sometimes people act as if she can do no wrong and he can do no right.

I kind of feel bad for Norbert, and I bet deep down a few other kids do too.

Well, anyway, guess what?

Today is Mom and Dad's anniversary. I want to do something nice for them. But I don't have any money to buy a present, or any clay or feathers or beads to make one.

If I were home, I'd bake a cake.

Mom and Dad are taking an extra long time getting dressed, so I gave Matt one of my postcards of the World's Biggest Church and put Lily's address on it. It's easy to remember her address—it's practically the same as ours because we live in the same apartment building.

Since Matt can't really write, he drew a picture of the Leaning Tower of Pisa with him and DogDog waving under it. Matt was concentrating hard. I could tell because his tongue was poking out of his mouth. The card came out well, though.

Just call me the World's Best Sister. W.B.S.?

I was thinking about working on my poem, but Dad says we have to do some "exploring."

When my family isn't worrying me, they're hurrying me!
Best wishes,

Melanie the W. B. S.

bedtime 🕐 at the hotel

Dear Diary,

Lullaby, Dreamer, Romie, Purr Purr, Sunshine, Blacky, and Collie are the names Matt and I gave to the cats napping around the Colosseum. Matt picked Blacky and Collie. I didn't think Blacky was very original, and I thought Collie would be better for a dog, but I did not call Matt *stupido* or Matt the Brat.

I'm trying to be nicer to Matt. So's Mom. She's kissing and hugging him extra. I accused her of kissing and hugging him more than me, and she did not even deny it. She just said, "That's because he lets me, Melanie."

I guess she has a point. It's true that when we cross a busy street, I sort of want her to hold my hand but I sort of hate it when she does.

Anyway, the Colosseum is so enormous, it's . . . colossal! Imagine if Yankee Stadium somehow got dissolved until the only thing left was a stone skeleton of a stadium with different wrecked-up layers. Dad said the Colosseum is where Romans held sports events, like gladiator contests and slaves fighting lions and prisoners fighting wild beasts. Sometimes it got filled up with water for boat battles. Sometimes fifty thousand people came to watch the fights and stuff.

Mom pointed out a section of the Colosseum that had columns that were "fine examples of Corinthian, Ionic, and Doric."

Matt said, "Dorky?"

Mom said, "Doric!" and looked at Dad to share one of their "Aren't our children adorable?" moments.

But Dad wasn't paying attention, so she said, "Marc, what are you looking at?"

It was as if Dad were in another world.

Mom said, "Marc, *whom* are you looking at?"

Mom likes to speak correctly.

Dad mumbled, "Sophia," and I saw Mom look over at this lady in a little blue sundress.

"Sophia?" Mom repeated. "Are you *sure?*"

"Who's Sophia?" I asked.

"Someone Dad knew a long time ago," Mom said.

"Who?" Matt asked.

"An old friend," Mom said, but the way she said it made me not quite believe her.

"Sophia!" Dad called out.

She turned around. She was really pretty. Her sundress was cut low up top, and she wore her sunglasses on top of her streaky blond hair like a headband.

She looked right at Dad, and her big brown eyes got even bigger, and she said Dad's name. It came out like "Marc?" and "Marc!" at the same time.

Dad walked toward her, and she walked toward him, and Dad smiled and gave her a big hug. She hugged him right back and kept her hand on his arm.

I didn't like this. I could tell Mom didn't either. Especially on their anniversary.

"You look great!" Dad said. "You haven't changed a bit."

Sophia giggled and said, "You look great too." She introduced another lady as her cousin Karen and added, "How long has it been? A dozen years?"

"More," Dad said. "Miranda and I have been married thirteen."

"Thirteen *today*." Mom shook their hands. I could tell she was on her best behavior. As a teacher, she has to be nice to lots of people she doesn't really like. Especially on Parents' Night and on the first and last days of school. But I can always tell when she's smiling for real.

"Happy anniversary," Sophia said.

"I've heard a lot about you," Mom said. "Let's see. My favorite story might be the one about the night Marc bought twenty-one helium balloons for your surprise birthday party and hid them in the back of his car. But then you opened the trunk to get something, and the balloons all flew away."

Sophia and Dad laughed and laughed.

How come I had never heard that story?

"What are you doing in Italy?" Sophia asked.

"We're taking a family vacation," Dad said.

"These are my *bambini*." I was wondering if he was showing off his kids or his Italian.

"We're having a honeymoon," Matt said, and smiled sort of cutely. He still has all his baby teeth.

"How about you?" Mom asked Sophia.

"I live here." She turned to Dad. "I've lived in Europe ever since we broke up."

Broke up? They used to go out?? I tried to picture them together but it was impossible. Im Po See Bee Lay.

Sophia said it was Karen's first trip to Rome, and she was showing her the sights. "She lives in the States," she said. That's what Italians call the United States.

Mom asked Karen where, and she said New York, and we found out she lives pretty near us.

"Why don't you join us for lunch?" Dad asked.

I bet Mom wanted to slug him.

Next thing you know, we all went to *La Dolce Vita* (La Dole Chay Vee Ta), which means The Sweet Life, which it was before Sophia and Karen started tagging along.

I mean, I liked when it was just our family.

We all sat down, and everyone ordered. Matt and I ordered spaghetti, and Mom ordered risotto (mushy rice), and Dad ordered gnocchi (potato dumplings). The waiter left, and Dad was staring at Sophia, and Mom was staring at Dad staring at Sophia. Karen was asking Matt about action figures and said, "Did you know that the Ninja Turtles—Michelangelo, Leonardo, Donatello, and Raphael—were named for Italian artists?"

"Cool," Matt said. Cool? I would have told her that Ninja Turtles are totally out.

The grown-ups were dipping their bread in olive oil and saying how good it was. In Italy, people like to talk about virgin things. Like the Virgin Mary. And extra virgin olive oil.

"What do you do here?" Mom asked Sophia, just to be nice.

"I restore paintings." She started explaining her job. "Some paintings are so old that they chip or peel. Others are damaged by water or dust. Or even earthquakes—like the one in 1997 in Assisi."

She was looking right at me, and I was trying to be polite and meet her eyes, but I wanted her to know I was on Mom's side. As an art teacher, Mom may have been interested in all this, but as a wife, Mom probably wanted Sophia to take a hike.

Especially today, on the anniversary of Mom and Dad's wedding day.

"I'm lucky. I love my work," Sophia was saying. "I get to restore masterpieces. I work very slowly and carefully to try to make a cracked or dingy painting look the way it did when the artist finished it. For instance," she asked me, "did you see the Sistine Chapel?"

I nodded. I didn't want to tell her that I practically had it memorized.

"Well, for a long time the colors were dull," Sophia continued. "Sort of brownish. But specialists from all over the world removed the centuries of soot and grime and brought back its initial brightness and grandeur. Together, we fixed it and cleaned it, centimeter by centimeter, inch by inch. It took thirteen years." She glanced toward Dad and sat up straight, all proud of herself.

"Cool," Matt said.

Traitor. I whispered for him to keep quiet because Mom might be feeling jealous of Sophia.

"What do you mean?" Matt whispered back.

"Sophia and Dad used to go out," I explained quietly.

"Go out where?" Matt asked.

I was about to say, "Forget it, you moron—you wouldn't understand," but instead I patiently said, "They used to be boyfriend and girlfriend."

Matt opened his eyes really wide, like that was about the last thing he expected me to say.

It *is* weird. If Dad and Sophia had gotten married, Matt and I wouldn't be here. We wouldn't have even been born!

My spaghetti came, and before I could stop him, the waiter sprinkled parmesan cheese all over it. And the thing is, it tasted amazingly okay.

The waiter gave Dad his dumplings, and Dad looked up at Sophia and said, "Hey, gnocchi and *occhi* rhyme." Which means dumplings and eyes rhyme. Which is true, because you say "Nyo Key" and "Oh Key."

But first of all, that isn't exactly a great poem. And second of all, since when did Mr. Lawyer become Mr. Poet?

I'm the one who is supposed to be writing thirty lines of poetry.

Anyway, Sophia was telling Dad that art restoration skills used to be passed on from fathers to sons but now more and more women are in on the action. She also told us stories about Michelangelo, only she doesn't call him "Michael Ann Jello." She calls him "Me Kay Lon Jay Lo." (She probably thinks her way is cooler.)

Well, however you say it, he had an enemy who insulted his ceiling, so, years later, when Michelangelo painted *The Last Judgment*, he painted the enemy's face right on one of the bad people that Jesus was sending to h—ll!

Dad laughed and laughed about that.

She and Dad were definitely laughing and smiling more than normal.

It seemed like flirting. I was wondering if Mom was feeling jealous of Sophia, and maybe even extra jealous since Sophia gets to fix up masterpieces whereas Mom only gets to look at them.

I had to do something.

Sophia may like to fix broken things, but I wanted her to know that her romance with my dad was gone for good, over and done with, peeled, cracked, and beyond repair.

I know my mom and dad argue once in a while, but they love each other. Their marriage is built on solid ground, not sandy clay. And even though Dad sometimes gets mad and grumpy, and I sometimes get mad and grumpy back, I wouldn't want him to go off and live in *Roma* or anything.

Mom keeps telling me that at my age, I'm not expected to take care of cars or wallets or even Matt. But she doesn't realize that I want to save the day.

I was a little nervous, but I raised my glass of water and did something I'd never done in my whole entire life.

"I call for a toast," I said. The grown-ups all stopped talking and looked right at me. "Here's to Mom and Dad on their thirteenth anniversary. To

Marc and Miranda—the World's Best Parents and the World's Best Couple."

Everyone clinked glasses and toasted Mom and Dad.

"Thirteen! *Tredici!*" Sophia said, pronouncing it Tray Dee Chee. "That's a lucky number in Italy."

Mom winked and gave me a big real smile.

And I handed Sophia my camera and asked her to take a picture of us—Mom and Dad and Matt and me.

The four M's.

Forever Yours,
Melanie the
Hero

Happy Anniversary

afternoon in the Car
..

Dear Diary,

Today is our last whole day in Italy. Tomorrow we go home. It will be a daytime flight, so we won't have to sleep on the plane, but Mom says that when we arrive in New York it will feel like bedtime even though it will be afternoon. I told her it may feel late, but I'll still want to order in beef and broccoli.

I miss Chinese food so much I won't even mind having to set the table and put away the dishes. Matt says that what he misses is cinnamon buns, but I think he just likes saying the word "buns."

Mom wanted to go to one last museum today.

I said, "Me and Matt don't want to."

Mom said, "Mean Matt?" which is her teachery way of correcting my grammar.

I said, "Matt *and I* don't want to go."

But then Mom pleaded and said we'd be quick, and we could go to the gift shop *first* and pick out any postcard we wanted, and the kids could race the parents through the museum to find the subjects of the postcards.

"Like a treasure hunt?" Matt asked.

"Exactly," Mom said.

"Okay, but let's all stick together," Matt said. He held Mom's hand and added, "I want us to live together forever and for always."

Mom said, "We'll always be a family, but someday you and Melanie will probably live on your own."

Matt said, "I don't want to live on my own. I want to stay with you."

Mom said, "I don't mean now. I mean someday when you're a grown-up, you might want to have your own home."

Matt was quiet. Then he said, "Mom, when I'm a grown-up, if I tell you I want to live by myself in my own home, will you remind me that I really don't?"

Mom just ruffled Matt's hair, and we went to the Capitoline Museum gift shop.

While we were choosing postcards, I overheard Mom tease Dad, "Do you still like her?"

I knew she meant Sophia.

"Not like I like you," Dad said, and he kissed Mom right on the lips. (Ewwww.)

Dad asked, "How about you? You still have a thing for David?"

Mom snuggled up to Dad and said, "I always will."

Dad just laughed, because who cares if your wife likes another man if that man is made of marble?

The postcard Matt picked out was of an ancient bronze boy trying to get a thorn out of his foot. Matt showed it to a guard, who showed Matt where to find it.

Matt led the way, and we all liked the boy. Dad said, "I guess kids have been stepping on thorns for thousands of years. Cave men and cave boys probably stepped on thorns."

"And cave women and cave girls," I added. "Now let's find my postcard." I'd picked out a female wolf nursing two human baby boys. I showed it to a different guard, and she pointed the way and we found it. According to Dad's guidebook, the wolf is over 2500 years old!

According to a legend, two baby boys, Romulus and Remus, got dumped by their father, Mars, on the bank of the river Tiber. They would have starved to death except that a mother wolf nursed and adopted them—kind of like what happened to Mowgli in *The Jungle*

Book, and sort of like what happened to Tarzan in *Tarzan*, except that he got saved by monkeys, not wolves. Anyway, Romulus and Remus grew up and founded a city. But they got into a big fight, and Romulus ended up killing Remus. And that's why the capital of Italy is named Rome, not Reme.

Well, Matt and I may have sibling rivalry, but at least we'd never kill each other!

On our way out of the museum, I showed Matt an old statue of a sad man whose nose was chipped off.

"Guess why he's so upset," I whispered.

"Why?"

"Because look what else is missing." I pointed to where his you-know-what should have been.

Matt and I cracked up.

Next we went to the bathroom. Mom and Dad didn't have to go, so Mom made me take Matt to the ladies' room. Matt can get too silly in ladies' rooms, but he acted normal, and he even taught me his trick for never getting burned with the C-is-for-Hot water. He said to remember that F is for Freezing.

Next stop: the Pantheon. Matt kept saying, "Look up!" and I kept thinking that if I did, he'd laugh and say, "Made you look." But when I finally did look up, Matt didn't laugh. He just said, "Isn't that awesome?"

The Pantheon is almost 2000 years old, and it has a big wide dome and no windows, and the only light comes from a hole at the top. Dad said it's called the Eye of God. In Italy, it seems as if God is always watching you.

Dad said that we wouldn't be able to see all the sites but that they'd saved one of the coolest things for last. So now we're driving to the *Santa Maria della Concezione* (San Ta Ma Ree Ya Day La Cone Chate See Own Ay).

It doesn't sound cool. It sounds like one more church.

By the way, if my handwriting is sloppy, it's because I'm writing in the car. I'm lucky I can read and write in cars. Matt says he can't even look at a book in a car or he'll throw up all over the place. I don't know if that's true or not, but I don't plan to hand him a book and find out. Could be messy.

xoxo,
Melanie.

same day
back in the <u>Car</u>

Dear Diary,

Dad was right. We just saw the coolest thing!!!

We visited these rooms that are a cemetery for around 4000 monks. Living monks took the dead monks' bones, and instead of burying them, they *decorated* with them. They glued them all over the walls in fancy designs. Like a humongous arts-and-crafts project!

There are tons of skulls and a bunch of complete skeletons. Wearing monks' robes. Staring at you, but with no eyes.

Matt could hardly believe they were actual people bones.

Even the ceilings were decorated with bones bones bones.

In the very last room, there was a sign written in different languages. It said:

> *What you are, we were.*
> *What we are, you will be.*

I bought five postcards.

It would be so cool to have a Halloween party there, but Mom said it's not for parties. I think it gave my parents the willies, and they were afraid it was too creepy for us. It did scare Matt a little. Not me. I like that it was spooky.

It makes you appreciate being alive, you know? I'm even appreciating my family, which is pretty weird. I mean, I might mention it to Miss Sands, but I won't tell Cecily or anything.

Faithfully,

Melanie

same day

bedtime  at the hotel

Dear Diary,

I just looked in the mirror, and I can't believe that besides crooked bangs and crooked teeth, my eyebrow looks crooked because of the stitches.

At least my glasses sort of hide it.

For dinner, we had pasta—surprise, surprise. Matt asked for penne—those little noodle tubes—because he likes to blow through them as if they were baby straws. I ordered spaghetti, and Mom and Dad nearly fainted when I asked for parmesan cheese on top. Dad said, "Look who's growing up" and gave me a big smile.

I can't believe I like parmesan cheese.

I can't believe we're going home tomorrow.

I can't believe we've been so far away.

I can't believe I still haven't written my poem.

That stupid poem! If I have a nightmare tonight, it won't be about skeletons, it will be about poetry.

*unpoetically
yours,
Melani*

March 29
morning in the hotel

Dear Diary,

You know what Matt told me last night after I turned out the light? He told me that even though he doesn't really know how to write yet (well, he *can* scrawl his name in capital letters), he's sure I can write anything.

"What do you mean?" I asked. How does Matt know how well I can write if he can't even read, if he can just sound out and guess?

"I mean," Matt said, "I'm sure you're a great writer."

"You said my poems were stupid."

"Mellie," Matt said in the dark, "all you ever do is write. In the hotel, in the car, on the train, at restaurants, in churches. You're always scribbling. You've practically filled up your diary. If you try, I know you can write a really good poem."

"You think so?"

"I'm positive," he said. "You'll do it on the plane."

"I hope you're right" was all I could say.

Matt does have a point. I do like to write, so maybe I'm making too big a deal of this poem thing. I'll just get lots of scrap paper and sharpened pencils and do it on the way back home. I've already begun, after all. It may not be a perfect start, but the Leaning Tower of Pisa didn't have a perfect start, and people like it.

The flight is eight hours. We leave around twelve, but we get to New York at around three. Mom says we'll go right to bed (after the Chinese dinner). She also says that at first we'll be rising and shining with the roosters but that in a few days we'll be back to normal.

Back to normal? I can't picture ever going totally back

to normal. Back to when Matt got on every last one of my nerves. Back to when parmesan cheese grossed me out. Back to when I thought doing acrobatics in the hotel was a bright idea.

One thing I like about Rome is that new stuff and old stuff are all mixed together. You see ancient ruins next to *gelato* stores, because cities change little by little, just like people do. So maybe instead of going back to normal, I'll be the old Melanie and the new Melanie mixed together.

All the best,

MiXed-up Mel

on board the

Dear Diary,

We're in the air. I remembered to go to the bathroom at the airport. Good thinking, right?

Outside I see clouds clouds clouds. Matt and I are next to each other again, and Mom and Dad are across the aisle.

I can't wait to get home and order beef with broccoli and turn on the TV and play on the computer and call Cecily and invite her over so we can bake muffins or make potions or microwave marshmallows. Maybe we can even have a sleepover—or a stay-up-over!

I'm excited to go home, but I can't believe I have school tomorrow, and I'm sorry to leave Italy. I hope I'll go back someday. Next time I'll ride a gondola in Venice and visit the city where Columbus was born.

This morning while Mom and Dad packed, they let Matt and me watch TV. It was funny to hear Popeye speak Italian. Then Mom said, "*Andiamo*" (On Dee Ahm Oh), which means "Let's go." But I couldn't find Hedgehog. Mom opened all the drawers and Dad checked behind all the doors, and he found her, all snug in my closet.

I held her tight, and Matt held DogDog, and we went down to the lobby. I was hoping to see Giorgio, but he wasn't there. Then we got in a taxi and said, "*Arrivederci, Italia!*" Ah Ree Veh Dare Chee means good-bye.

At the airport, signs everywhere said *Vietato Fumare*

(Vee Ay Ta Toe Foo Mar Ay), which means No Smoking. But people were smoking anyway. Everywhere there were No Smoking signs and smoking people. Disgusting! People smoke too much in Italy. The restaurants don't even have No Smoking sections!

I was thinking about reporting the smokers to a nearby policeman, since we're already friends with half the policemen in Italy. But then I noticed that even the policeman was smoking!

It's pretty *ridicolo* (Ree Dee Co Lo). That's Italian for ridiculous.

We checked our luggage and showed our passports, and Dad gave us thousands of *lire* to spend before the plane took off. Thousands! Over ten dollars each! You see, you can take Italian money to an American bank and change *lire* into dollars, but banks charge for that, so Mom and Dad figured what the heck, let's just blow it at the airport duty-free shop. Duty-free means no taxes. Like: Everything's on sale! Plus, it was our last chance to buy souvenirs. And Mom says she owes me some back allowances.

Which she does. Big time.

Anyway, Mom and Dad bought these gross dried-up porcini mushrooms and also this bottle of green liqueur with a fig in the middle of it. Yuck. We'll get home and they'll invite people over for dried mushrooms and fig liqueur. I bet even grown-ups would rather have hot dogs and soda.

Hot dogs. I almost forgot about hot dogs. I'm glad America has hot dogs. And Chinese food. And chili. And bagels. I wrote another two-liner in my head:

I'm just about ready
To give up Spaghetti.

With the last of the *lire*, Matt bought three key rings for his backpack. I helped pick them out.

I bought postcards. At first, to my naked eye, all the postcards seemed to be of Rome. But I looked behind the front ones and saw postcards of other cities too. There were even postcards of the whole *Birth of Venus* and the whole *David*, so I bought those to show just Cecily. (Not to show my classmates!!!)

I also bought chocolate. *Cioccolato* (Cho Co La Toe). Another important Italian word.

The chocolate I bought is called Baci (Bah Chee), which means kisses. If you don't mind hazelnuts, Baci are better than Hershey's Kisses.

Speaking of kisses, Mom and Dad are in a good mood and are drinking airplane champagne again. Last night they said they were happy Matt and I are getting along so well. Well, we're happy *they* are getting along so well!

In the airport, Dad even complimented Mom on her Italian and said she sounds better than ever. He said she is good at Romance languages and at romance. Mom just smiled.

And get this: Mom ended up being glad she met Sophia, because Sophia promised Mom lots of art posters and slides and books that she can use for teaching. Karen said she'd bring them to New York when she returns next week.

Mom started working on this funny quiz for her students called "Are You Art Smart?" She says she doesn't like to give killer tests because the point of art isn't to memorize facts but to see things in new ways. She says you learn more by making art than by taking tests. So far, here are her questions:

1. Michelangelo's most famous sculpture is named
a. *Stu* **b.** *Jimmy* **c.** *David*

2. Which Italian artist painted the *Mona Lisa?*
a. Lisa Mona **b.** Leonardo da Vinci
c. Leonardo DiCaprio

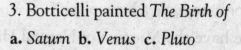

3. Botticelli painted *The Birth of*
a. *Saturn* **b.** *Venus* **c.** *Pluto*

We got them all right, but Matt said, "You should make Uranus a wrong answer."

Mom said, "Uranus?"

Matt said, "Not *my* anus. Uranus!" and cracked up.

Mom said, "I'm not in the mood, Matt."

Matt said, "You *should*, Mom."

Mom said, "I'll think about it," which means no.

I'm going to stop writing in my diary now and start

writing that poem. Matt's right. It can't be that big a deal. I'll just plain do it.

Matt asked Dad what Italian tourists like to do in New York. Dad thought about it and said they like to go to the Statue of Liberty, the Metropolitan Museum of Art, Wall Street, Fifth Avenue, Central Park, maybe the Metropolitan Opera, maybe Chinatown and Little Italy, and definitely the Empire State Building—which Matt used to call the Entire State Building.

Matt said, "Don't we have a bone place?"

Dad said, "We have the Museum of Natural History."

I really should write that poem. Miss Sands says I'm good at stalling. She calls it procrastinating.

I'm glad I have the window seat again.

I checked the map of Europe in my airline magazine. It shows Holland, Spain, France, England, Ireland, and a whole lot of other countries I wouldn't mind visiting someday.

☺   ☺   ☺

A lady in front of Matt just got mad at him for kicking the back of her seat. So Matt stopped kicking, but he pressed the button that makes your seat lean way back, and the man behind him said, *"Basta!"* (Bah Sta), which means "Enough!"

Poor Matt. He needs to not make a nuisance of himself for eight hours. That's not easy for a little kid.

And he is a little kid. He can't help it. Just like I can't help being an E.B.S. every once in a while.

Dad just told him, "Why can't you sit still like Melanie? She's not causing any problems." (Hee hee.)

Maybe Matt will fall asleep. If he falls asleep with his mouth open again, I might take a picture. Right now he's coloring on barf bags. Mom showed him a brownish crayon called Burnt Sienna and said Siena is a city in Italy with earth and buildings exactly that color. I'd like to visit it someday too.

Hey, I just thought of another two-liner:

I don't mind my little brother,
But I would not want another.

Out the window I can see mountaintops! Maybe if I look closely I can see that Michelangelo marble.

Michelangelo lived to be almost ninety. Raphael and Caravaggio died young.

I admit I'm more curious about them now than I used to be. I might even let Mom take me to the Metropolitan Museum.

Might.

Or to the Frick Museum. Mom once said kids are not allowed to go until they're ten years old. Which I now am.

I hope there are no air pockets up here.

But maybe when you are going places, there are always pockets in the air or bumps in the road or thorns on the path.

Man, oh, man, I am a regular philosopher.

Unfortunately, I'm supposed to be a poet!

I've been doodling yin-yangs and peace signs and smiley faces, but it's rhyme time.

Thirty lines.

This could take hours.

I have hours.

130

Seven six five four three two one.
If I don't begin, I'll never be done.

I just came back from the bathroom, and I was going to ask Mom to play Hangman. I was going to try to stump her with "gypsy" or "lynx" because she always guesses the a e i o u vowels first. But one look at Mom, and I could tell she didn't want to play any games. She told me to "buckle up and buckle down."

So here I go. Ready or not.

From the one and only—

Melanie

still on board!

Dear Diary,

Hip hip hurray!

I did it!

I came up with thirty lines!

131

My Trip to Italy
by
Melanie Martin

We've been to Rome.

We're going home.

It's sad that I

Must say good-bye.

And so for now

I'll just say, "Ciao."

The cats were all cute

In Italy's boot.

The Colosseum was cool.

Each church was a jewel.

It's good Sistine's ceiling

Is no longer peeling.

I walked along narrow streets,

Italian shoes on my feets.

I liked the pizza and Uffizi,

But waiting on line was not too easy.
I liked Lucca's old stone walls.
I hope Pisa's tower never falls.

My family now has a motto.
It's this: "Who wants gelato?"
I learned a few Italian words.
Matt learned to chase Italian birds.
I'm glad for my father and my mother
And even for my little brother.

We're landing now—I'm out of time—
I better finish up my rhyme.
I feel lucky to be a Martin.
It's a fine family to have a part in.
Here comes the last line of this verse:
It's not Dante, but it could be worse!

Poetically yours,

Melanie
the
Magnificent

Dear Diary,

I showed my poem to Dad. I thought he'd say, "Good job." But he kind of snickered at some of the rhymes and pronounced the whole thing "Cute."

Cute?

Again?

I showed my poem to Mom. I can tell what Mom is thinking no matter what she says.

She read the poem and said, "You finished it. Thirty lines."

I knew that meant she thought it was dog doo.

"Why don't you like it?" I asked.

"I do like it, Melanie."

She stayed quiet, so I said,

I'm NOT A Poet
AND I KNOW IT.

Mom smiled. "Did Miss Sands say it had to rhyme?"

"No."

"What did she say?"

"She said to write thirty lines and to think about my family."

"I'll hold on to this poem. I won't lose it," Mom said. "But why don't you begin again? Poetry doesn't have to rhyme. It has to speak the truth."

"What? I'm not doing a new one! No way! That is *ridicolo!* I never said I was Emily Dickinson." I thought Mom would be impressed that I knew the Italian word for ridiculous *and* the name of a woman poet.

But Mom said, "Honey, your poem has a lot of charm. But since we still have several hours before landing—"

"C'mon, Mom. I admit that the word 'feets' was lame, and rhyming 'Martin' and 'part in' was pathetic, but—"

Mom looked straight at me, her mind made up. I could picture her calmly handing fresh clay or new paper to a student who she thought hadn't done his or her best work.

"Mom, it's the best I can do."

"I think you can do even better," Mom said. "You have

talent. You love to write. And you have a lot to say. Now, I'll take care of this poem while you start a new one."

This was so not fair. But how could I argue when she was saying nice things about me?

I rolled my eyes and mumbled, "I guess I don't have anything better to do up here."

Mom smiled a half smile.

Believe it or not, I'm back in my seat. At square one. Above the Atlantic. Between Europe and America. With the pressure on.

Wish me luck.

Yours,

Melani

still on board!

Dear Diary,

Whew! I kept writing and writing and counting and counting, and I copied over thirty lines right before landing. I don't know if my poem is any good, but Mom didn't ask to see it, so I didn't show it to her.

I did notice that Matt was gone for a long time, so I asked Mom and Dad, "Is Matt lost?"

Dad said, "How can you get lost on an airplane?"

Just then Matt came back. It turned out he had gotten stuck in the bathroom. He kept trying to turn the knob to open the door, but he forgot he also had to push the latch to unlock it.

We're going to land soon. Outside, the houses and bridges and buildings are getting bigger bigger bigger.

Yours,

Melani

3:30 on 3/30

at my desk in New York City

Dear Diary,

I just got back from school. In the morning I gave Miss Sands my poem, and in the afternoon she let me show my postcards and tell about my stitches and describe the Sistine Chapel, the Colosseum, and the bone church. I also talked about the pizza, pasta, and ice cream. And I gave everyone an Italian coin.

Everyone said, "Thank you," except Norbert. He said, "*Grazie*." I was surprised that he knew any Italian. The other kids started to make fun of him by repeating, "*Grazie*" sarcastically, but I looked right at him and said, "*Prego*," for "You're welcome." I think that over vacation he must have gotten his hair cut or something because it wasn't sticking up as much. Someday I'll have to ask him if he has a cousin who works as a bellhop in Rome.

Miss Sands handed me back my poem and asked if I would please read it out loud.

I said, "I'd rather not."

She said, "I'd like you to," in that same teacher tone Mom used on the airplane.

"It's embarrassing," I whispered.

Miss Sands whispered back, "This isn't about your reading it. It's about everyone else's hearing it."

It is so hard to argue with teachers!

"Go ahead," Miss Sands said. "Nice and loud."

My heart started pounding and my hands were sweaty and my throat got dry. I looked up at Cecily, and she mouthed, "Don't worry," and that made me feel a smidge better.

But I still said, "I don't know if I can."

"I know you can," Miss Sands said, waiting calmly. Just like Mom.

There was no way out. So I read my poem aloud:

I have been far away
But now I'm home.
I may look the same
But I am different.

I went to a country where
I didn't know anyone
And what I found was
My own family—
The ones I thought I knew,
The ones I took for granted.

What if my dad hadn't married my mom?
What if my brother had gotten lost for good?
What if all we ever did was fight,
When if we try
We can help each other,
Not hurt each other?

I saw skeletons in Italy.
I know I won't live forever.
But while I'm here,
I will try to work hard,
Like Michelangelo,
Because in some ways,
He never did die.

I will also try to be kinder
To the people
I hardly know and
The people I already love.
And I really hope I can
Keep taking trips and
Keep coming home.

At first no one said anything, and I could feel my face get beet red. But when I finally looked up, Miss Sands was beaming at me. Norbert, who is usually quiet, raised his hand and said he liked my poem.

I smiled and said, "*Grazie.*"

Nobody laughed.

Miss Sands beamed at the whole entire class.

Dear Diary,

I can't believe I'm on the very last pages of this new diary. I could call it *Melanie Martin's Month of March.* Or *How I Survived Matt the Brat, Michelangelo, and the Leaning Tower of Pizza.* I might even ask Mom for a new diary.

My family just came to say good night.

Nobody was in a hurry. Which was nice.

Dad was actually in an excellent mood because some honest Italian man found his travel wallet and mailed it to him. The money and cards were gone, but Dad's driver's license was in it (that's how the man knew our address) and so was the photo Dad likes of me holding baby Matt. Yippee!

Mom said, "Miss Sands told me she liked your poem."

(Teachers tell each other everything.)

Mom added, "She said it was quite mature."

"Mature?" Dad said. "The one about 'The cats are all cute in Italy's boot'?"

"I wrote a new one," I said, though to tell you the truth, I still like my old one every bit as much.

"You did?" Dad asked.

"Let's hear it," Matt said.

Dad sat on my rocking chair, and Mom sat on my bed, and Matt and DogDog sat on the floor. Matt stuck out his hand, and I knew that meant he was ready to give the poem a thumbs-up (for good), a thumbs-down (for dog poop), or a thumbs-sideways (for so-so).

I read my poem.

I peeked over at Matt's hand.

He was giving me a big thumbs-up. DogDog was giving me a big paws-up. "I knew you could do it," Matt said.

"Melanie, it's good," Mom said, and I could tell she meant it.

Even Dad seemed sort of impressed. "When did you write it?"

"On the plane."

"You're a good writer," he said.

"*Grazie*," I said.

Matt went back to his room, and Mom and Dad tucked me and Hedgehog in and kissed me good night.

"I'm proud of you, Precious," Mom said.

"I'm proud of you too, Mellie," Dad said.

I could tell they both meant it.

And you know what I just realized?

I'm proud of me three!

Ciao for now!

*Melanie
Martin*

ACKNOWLEDGMENTS!

Writing is a solitary task, but it is incredible—or *incredibile* (In Cray Dee Bee Lay)—how many people helped me with Melanie's journey. I want to thank my nine fellow travelers to Italy: Emme, Elizabeth, Robert, David, Cynthia, Eric, Mark, Marybeth, and Leighton. *Mille grazie* to my agent, Laura Peterson, and everyone at Knopf, especially Tracy Gates, Sarah Hokanson, and Simon Boughton. And heartfelt thanks to all the kids and grown-ups who kept me going—including David Nickoll, Vanessa and John Wilcox, Mary Lemons, Ed Abrahams, Elise Howard, Bonnie Beer, Katie Goldstein, Cathy Roos, James McMenamin, Warrie Price, Mimmola Girosi, Richard Firestone, Karen Lausa, Patty Dann, Evie Gurney, Matty Reategui, Helen Clougherty, Amber Gross, Ann Zeidner, Mike Wolmetz, Erin Arruda, David Roos, Marc and Charlie Aidinoff, and the Squam Lake Cousins. Thanks too to the helpful students at Trinity School, including Tara Rodman, Stephanie Jenkins, Leni Kirschenbaum, Sujata Gidumal, Anna Sakellariadis, Amanda Manocherian, and Ms. Jarecki's class of 2009.

This is **Carol Weston's** first novel. She has a B.A. in French and Spanish comparative literature from Yale and an M.A. in Spanish from Middlebury.

Carol Weston is the advice columnist for *Girls' Life* magazine. Her other books include *Girltalk: All the Stuff Your Sister Never Told You*; *For Girls Only: Wise Words, Good Advice*; and *Private and Personal: Questions and Answers for Girls Only*.

As a girl, Ms. Weston kept diaries. As a teenager, she made a small fortune by baby-sitting. Once she had enough money to buy plane tickets, she began to travel. Now she and her husband and their two daughters take trips together. But they always love to come back home to New York City.

You can visit the author at her Web site: www.carolweston.com.